Convergence- Book One:
Incarnation

Katherine E. Lewis & Rebecca Lewis

Convergence- Book One: Incarnation

Copyright © 2021 Katherine E. Lewis & Rebecca Lewis

theconvergencebooks.com

Cover Design by Allison Sanders

ISBN: 978-1-7377335-0-8

Printed in the United States of America

First Edition

In Memory of
Robert Felix Perkins
(Still the King)

PROLOGUE

"PLEASE, DARCY. PLEASE, no more."

His voice is a whisper, but he knows she can hear him. His fingers dig into the dirt beneath him, trying to gain purchase in the wet earth. The trees that had until tonight stood tall now lay flattened, forming the edges of the circle where William Rochester struggles to his knees. In the patches of moonlight, he sees fallen trees aren't the only corpses on the ground. His sob echoes in the unnatural silence of the dead.

He spots her near the tree line. The hair on the back of his neck stands on end. She steps into the clearing, a shadow but for her gray eyes glowing through the haze of destruction.

She closes the space between them, her eyes blazing brighter. A mist rolls in like an angry sea. Deep cold seizes his chest and radiates beneath his skin, into his muscles and down to his bones.

The moonlight illuminates her white hair and marble skin blue, and her lace dress floats as though suspended in water. A shimmering glow surrounds her, resembling light refracting off waves.

"They're all dead," he whispers. "It's over."

"It's over, Rochester," she says, her voice low. "For you."

She fixes him in her gaze, and the remaining breath leaves Rochester's lungs as she pulls in whatever life he has left. He closes his eyes, not wanting the last image he sees to be her.

"Stop!"

A warm wave of air cuts through the cold, forcing it back. Rochester's eyes fly open.

Ida strides into the clearing. Tall and sturdy, her dark hair trails behind her in untamed curls. Her face is streaked with tears, and her hands are stained with blood.

As Ida moves, the heat ebbs and flows around her, like the tide pulling waves to and from shore. She stops in front of Rochester. He gulps in the warmth that dissipates the cold clenching in his chest.

"I told you to leave," Darcy commands.

"And I said no," Ida says. "Enough, Darcy."

"I am not done," Darcy growls, the surrounding air reverberating.

The mist kicks up again, churning in the air.

"They're dead!" Ida yells.

"Not all of them! Not Rochester, not the cowards who ran!" Darcy screams, stepping toward her sister. "They should get away with what they did?"

"Darcy, please," Ida's voice cracks.

Rochester feels Ida's plea in his heart, so warm he fears it might combust.

"We're past that, Ida. You think you have the power to stop me?"

"It's not just about power."

The sky above them swirls with storm clouds, alive with

energy. Lightning crackles, pulsating the air in sharp relief, and a clap of thunder rumbles.

"You've broken every law of nature and the laws of our community," Ida says in a voice as fierce as her blue eyes. "You may have the power you took, but you have become untethered."

"Enough of the bedtime stories! I'm building a new future, and no one will stand in my way. Not even you."

Lightning rips through the clearing as the sisters release their might on one another. The two energy fields meet in full force, a crack sounding through the forest. The ground between them trembles, catches fire, freezes, and shatters.

Rochester watches in horror. "It's over," he whispers, releasing his last breath.

Across the county, a power outage hits that will last for weeks.

ONE

MERA AWOKE IN the passenger seat, gasping for air.

"Ahh!" the man driving cried, veering to the other side of the road.

Mera looked at her driver, Vince, who was stealing glances at her while maintaining an eye on the winding forest road. He had been on edge since he picked her up from the airport in Boston, considering her with equal parts apprehension and mild alarm. She gave him a weak thumbs up and turned to look out the window. They were driving through the same dense forest they had been traveling through since leaving the highway hours ago.

It was only a dream, she told herself, closing her eyes and pressing her forehead against the cool glass of the passenger window. She must have fallen asleep without noticing. It wasn't the first dream she'd had about her mother since the disappearance, but this dream had been . . . different.

Mera's stomach lurched again, but this time because Vince had slammed on the brakes. The car skidded to a halt in front of a driveway camouflaged by a leafy archway formed from the entwined limbs of two massive oak trees. Vince maneuvered the sedan through the tunnel of leaves, the emerald canopy brushing the roof of the car as they made their way up the drive.

They drove for a few minutes before they reached a locked gate blocking the road. Vince plucked a yellow sticky note with a series of numbers written on it from the manila file folder on the dashboard and hopped out of the car.

As he hurried toward the fence, Mera reached forward, picked up the folder, and flicked it open. She glanced at Vince, who was looking from the sticky note to the gate and scratching his head, then examined its contents.

MISSING: Kellen, Genevieve, 35, swam up to her from the copy of the police report. *Minor daughter*, Mera read, her eyes flickering over the page. *Abandoned.*

She closed the folder and tossed it back onto the dash right as Vince dropped himself into the car, panting from his battle with the gate. He glanced at the folder in disarray and then at Mera. With a huff, he threw the car into drive, and they proceeded.

Mera knew, of course, that the Phoenix police had decided early on that her mother had run away. She tried to explain something criminal must have happened, but Mera couldn't find anyone willing to do more than nod sympathetically. She was handed from caseworker to caseworker, all the way to Vince, now eager to leave her on the doorstep of the long-lost grandmother they had discovered in Convergence, Maine. A grandmother Mera had never even known existed.

The trees thinned as the driveway inclined, and a massive house came into view.

The Victorian house on the oceanside cliff reminded Mera

of the covers of the gothic romance novels her mother used to borrow from the library, its facade equal parts graceful curves and sharp edges, its color dulled to a haunted gray. A sturdy tower rose from its right side, and a porch wrapped around the front. Wispy clouds drifted by the weathervane on the roof.

Vince and Mera exited the car, and Vince made his way to wrestle Mera's suitcase from the trunk. Mera closed her eyes and took a deep breath of the salty Maine air, brisk though it was still August. She gathered up her dark red hair and tucked it into her sweatshirt, pulling the hood closer around her neck. She could hear the ocean beyond the cliff and shuddered at the sound, remembering her dream.

The front door of the house creaked open a few inches. The afternoon light shadowed the veranda, making it so Mera could discern only a figure standing in the doorway.

"Ahh, good, that must be your grandmother!" Vince squinted toward the house, still tugging at the suitcase. He raised his voice to speak into the shadows of the porch. "Mrs. Kellen, I'm Vince. We spoke on the phone."

He paused here as if he expected confirmation, but there was only silence. He waited a few beats and pressed on. "There's this paperwork, and if I could use your bathroom—"

"No," a voice from the shadows boomed. "Leave the paperwork and go."

Vince hesitated for a moment, the command still rebounding off the veranda. "Sounds good!" he said, pulling the suitcase free. He came around the front of the car and dropped the suitcase at Mera's feet with a dull thud.

"Wait, really?" Mera balked. "You're not going to do an

inspection or whatever?"

"Well, everything seems in order, doesn't it?" Vince said, waving his hand vaguely toward the house. He rummaged around the car before pulling out a second, much thinner manila folder than the one on the dashboard. He thrust it toward Mera.

"These are the documents for your grandmother. She can mail them," he said to Mera. He backed toward his car door and opened it behind him. "My card is in there. Good luck!"

Vince slammed his car door shut and drove out of sight, his sedan swallowed up by the forest through which they had come.

Mera turned around and took in the entire house, feeling smaller and smaller the further up her eyes traveled. She wasn't ready to go inside and meet this mystery grandmother whom her mother had never mentioned. The woman who was so disinterested in meeting her granddaughter that she wouldn't even come outside to greet her. And unfortunately, the woman who represented Mera's final, desperate hope in convincing someone to help her save her mother.

Mera sighed as she gripped the handle of her heavy suitcase and walked toward the mystery that was her grandmother's house.

TWO

AS SOON AS Mera shut the front door behind her, she wished she hadn't. Inside, the curtains were drawn, making the house so dark, she couldn't see which way to go. She was going to call out when a light from a chandelier flickered on far above her, illuminating the cavernous foyer.

An older woman stood with her hand on the light switch. Graceful and imposing, she had long silver hair cascading in loose ringlets down her shoulders. She wore a silken, steel-colored blouse tucked into pleated trousers and an impatient look on her face.

"Uh, hello," Mera attempted after an uncomfortable beat. Her voice echoed to the high ceiling. "Guess you're my grandmother?"

"Ida," her grandmother replied before she turned on her heel and strode down the hallway. Mera hurried to follow, only having a second to glimpse an ornate, curved stairway and four sets of French doors leading off the hall.

Portraits of women in varying shades of blue lined the walls in wooden frames, their faces soft and blurred as Mera passed them. But one stopped her—a woman with intense, metal-gray eyes, a delicate strand of white hair framing her striking face.

"That's impossible," Mera whispered to herself.

Mera was in a lush clearing, a place she had never been but felt familiar. She turned to see her mother standing on the edge of a cliff overlooking the ocean, her dark hair loose in the ocean breeze. As Mera walked toward her mother, a pain gripped her center, doubling her over.

"Mom," Mera cried out. "Help me."

As Mera looked up at the woman before her, she realized it wasn't her mother. The woman's dark hair was streaked with white, and her silver eyes danced in their metallic luminance.

Mera's core lurched, and a rising tide began pushing its way up through her chest and into her throat, moving to meet the ocean in the woman's gaze.

"Don't," Mera had begged.

The woman smiled as Mera was lifted from the ground and into the air.

"It's time to wake up, dear," the woman whispered.

The woman waved her hand, and Mera flew off the edge of the cliff.

This plummeting sensation had jolted her awake in Vince's car, shocking him into almost steering them off the road.

The woman now stared at Mera through the canvas. Her stomach lurched once more, pulling at her center like water being dragged back to sea. *It had been a dream . . . right?*

As Mera stepped closer, drawn by the pull of the woman's swimming eyes, Ida cleared her throat.

"No touching," she scolded.

"Who's this?" Mera asked, breaking from her reverie, but Ida swept from the spot and crossed into the kitchen. Mera hurried to keep up, casting one backward glance at the mysterious woman in blue. She entered the kitchen and observed the room was bigger than the apartment she had shared with her mother in Phoenix.

Exposed wood beams traveled up the walls and onto the ceiling. The dark marble counters gleamed as bright as the stone-tiled floors. Even the antique appliances looked new, having been well-preserved.

"This kitchen is to stay as clean as you see it. I will cook, so I can't imagine you'll need the kitchen often. Let's move along," Ida said, and Mera followed her into another hallway.

They stopped outside a room with a locked door.

"This room is my private study and off limits. Do you understand?" Ida rasped her knuckles on the door to punctuate her question.

Mera nodded, confident she could begrudge the irritable old recluse her secret room.

And so, they continued. They raced through a conservatory made of glass walls and wild-looking plants. Next, they breezed through the library with wall-to-ceiling shelves of faded books, followed by a peek at the music room with a grand piano and a glimpse of an elaborate dining room.

Then came a drawing room, a sitting room, a morning room, and a family room, each with furniture arranged around marble fireplaces. Ida deemed them all to be less relevant to Mera than the one before it.

As they moved to the second floor, the doors opened to

reveal made-up guest bedrooms and closets filled with expensive-looking linens.

Mera had the sense that she was touring an immaculate dollhouse.

On the third floor, Ida stopped in front of the only room she imagined Mera might find useful.

"And this will be your bedroom. Please make a list of any personal items you need. Dinner is in one hour in the dining room," Ida stated, turning to walk away.

"Wait!" Mera exclaimed.

Ida revolved on the spot to face her again.

"I was hoping we could . . ." Mera began, then paused, unsure what to say next.

Discuss my mother's disappearance? Or my dream about Portrait Lady? Mera thought to herself.

"Never mind," Mera finished.

"See you at dinner then." Ida disappeared downstairs.

Mera walked into her new room and closed the door behind her. She took in the mahogany furniture, the vase with real flowers on the bedside table, and the tall windows set into the wall with plush window seats. The silver threads in the seafoam wallpaper caught the afternoon light and danced across the walls like glittering waves. Mera crossed to the windows and saw her room looked over the cliffs and ocean.

She threw herself onto the window seat bench with a sigh. She was with the family she always hoped she had but was more alone than ever. Instead of the warmth and belonging she had longed for, she found herself trapped in the museum of her mother's childhood, thousands of miles away from her last known whereabouts.

She pressed her forehead against the cool glass window, closed her eyes, and let the worry rock against her like the waves below her.

***

Mera wasn't sure how long she had stayed curled up on the window seat, watching the late afternoon sky cycle through its watercolor palette. Though Mera's body yearned for sleep, her mind would not rest. It hadn't slowed its racing for one moment since the night her mother disappeared.

She began reciting what she knew, something she did often. Her mom had left for work that Thursday morning three weeks ago as Mera got up for school. They shouted goodbye at one another as Mera shuffled from her bedroom into the narrow shotgun apartment hallway. Her last glimpse of her mother was her dark hair billowing behind her as she hurried out the front door.

But Mera's mother never came home. An hour past her typical arrival time, Mera picked up the phone to call the bank where her mother worked and saw a new voice message. Mera pressed play and her stomach dropped—it was from her mother's work hours earlier. Genevieve had never even arrived.

The police conducted their so-called investigation. Mera lost count of how many times she insisted her mother didn't have a boyfriend to skeptical police officers. Detectives turned up no leads.

"And you're sure she never told you anything about this alleged absent father of yours?" the detective assigned to her mother's case had pressed during their last meeting, disbelief etched on his features.

"I'm sure," Mera repeated, her cheeks burning.

The case was closed. Their official theory? She had run away—vanishing without a trace.

In the darkening light of the bedroom, familiar panic rose in Mera's chest again. Her mother was out there somewhere, in danger. Ida might help, but their first meeting hadn't been convincing. But maybe dinner would go better. What other choice was there?

Mera's stomach stirred, but it had nothing to do with hunger. It was the same feeling she'd had ever since she arrived in Convergence and was thrown off the cliff in her dream by the woman with the white streak of hair. It was impossible to dream of this woman and then find her portrait hanging downstairs.

Unless it wasn't a dream, a voice in her mind prodded.

Mera stood and shook her head to clear the thought. She took one last bracing breath and then she made her way downstairs for dinner.

***

After a few wrong turns, Mera found the dining room. As she pushed the large oak doors open, she stopped, frozen in the entryway, unprepared for the grandeur that greeted her on the other side.

Each wall hosted a different panel, stretching to the high ceilings of the first floor. Opposite the doorway, floor-to-ceiling windows lined the wall. There were delicate designs etched in the windowpanes—an hourglass, a leaf in the wind, wingless people flying through the sky. The etchings twinkled in the warm light of the chandelier, set across the glass in shimmering motion.

To her right, a massive fireplace of sturdy red brick sat beneath a charcoal drawing of the sun, its rays extending like vines and reaching to the ground. People climbed on each vine, their free hands outstretched toward the sun.

On the wall to the left were several stone panels featuring an intricate tree carving, the roots protruding in braided ropes. The tree was made of tiny people, intertwined as one.

Mera turned to the last wall, an elaborate fountain installation with water cascading from the top. Embedded into the fountain was a circle of blown-glass figurines. Made of blue and green sea glass, the figures resembled elongated droplets of water, with long arms reaching out to the figurines on either side of them. The water flowed between the figurine's outstretched arms, making it appear to pass between them in an unbroken chain.

With a surge of familiarity, Mera recognized the figurines in the fountain. Her mother had the same delicate trinkets on her bedside table. Mera drew closer to the figurines, watching the water pass between them as though in a trance.

"The food is getting cold," Ida's voice cut into Mera's thoughts.

Mera staggered backward, turning to look at Ida. She sat with her back to Mera, eating her dinner. It struck Mera how strange it was for Ida to surround herself with these depictions of community when she seemed so solitary. She saw a plate laid out for her across the table.

"Thank you," Mera said.

Ida nodded before cutting into her chicken.

The two ate in silence.

So much for sparkling conversation, Mera thought. She set

down her fork, preparing herself to break the silence. When she looked up at Ida, she had her grandmother's full attention.

"Yes?" Ida asked expectantly.

"My mom never talked about you," Mera blurted out. "Why is that?"

Ida froze and looked at her plate again.

"You would have to ask your mother," Ida said after a moment.

"Well, that's tough, what with her vanishing and all."

Ida looked up at Mera, her expression stony. "I'm afraid I don't have any answers for you. I haven't spoken to your mother since the last time she vanished."

Mera stared hard across the table at her grandmother. Her mind raced, trying to piece together the fragments her mother had let slip of her estrangement from Ida. All she knew was her mother left home and cut ties.

"Something is wrong," Mera said. "She would never just leave me. Is there anyone else she might contact? Someone in our family?"

Ida stood from her chair, gathering her dishes. "There is no one else."

Mera had hoped that if she hadn't known about Ida, there could be more family she might not know. Someone who could be a haven for her mother. But now, she knew. . . . There was no one else.

"You would do well to go to sleep early tonight. You have school in the morning," Ida stated. "We'll leave at 7:15."

Mera just nodded as Ida walked out of the room, but then Ida stopped.

Without turning to look at Mera, she asked, "Your mother

told you nothing, then? About . . . anything?"

Mera looked up at her grandmother. The word *anything* rang in her ears.

"No," Mera replied.

Ida swept from the room, the dishes rattling in her hands.

THREE

THE FUZZY NUMBERS on the clock next to her bedside read 3:00 a.m. She had another three hours to sleep, but Mera's eyes swept around the dark bedroom, heart pounding in her chest. Something had startled her awake. She strained to listen, but the house was silent.

She stood and crept to the door, easing it open. As she crossed the threshold into the hallway, the air grew heavier. It enveloped her in a blanket of heat as she moved toward the staircase. Her heartbeat quickened as she descended the staircase with unknown purpose.

Mera found herself outside Ida's study, the forbidden room on the first floor. Light spilled out from the crack beneath the closed door. She heard Ida speaking in hushed tones.

"A danger to everyone," Mera thought Ida said.

She moved through the heavy air and brought her face closer to the door, listening. A second person responded. Was that a man's voice?

Mera pressed against the door to listen and realized the hot air filling the house was escaping from under the study door. It was pouring out of the crack and rolling over her feet in waves of heat. The hot air moved up her body, licking at her neck and warming her cheeks, filling her nostrils. It reminded Mera of being outside right before a storm.

Mera had to see beyond the door. She needed to understand this feeling in the air.

Before she reached for the doorknob, it turned on its own and the door opened. A blast of warm air billowed out. She peered inside the room.

There was Ida, her long silver hair flowing around her in the breeze. She was bent low over something on the table, her hands moving over the object, obscured by a shimmering heat.

Ida whipped around to face Mera, and their eyes met. Ida's eyes blazed an otherworldly blue, swirling like waves in a hurricane.

Mera sat upright in bed, gasping.

Her room was freezing, the cool ocean air pouring in from her open bedroom window. Her eyes darted around, but everything was calm in the early morning air.

A dream, she thought, closing her eyes and drawing in a deep breath as she lay back against the pillow. *Just a dream.*

What she had seen was impossible. Mera shivered, unable to shake the memory of the intensity of her grandmother's eyes, the intoxicating heat, the mystery man's voice.

She rolled out of bed and closed the open window. Even if the dream was a product of her tired mind, she wasn't eager to lock eyes with her grandmother again.

The clock clicked over to 6:30 a.m., and the alarm blared. It was time to get ready for her next trial. High school.

***

"You should have breakfast," Ida said, her face buried in a newspaper, as Mera entered the kitchen. "We'll leave in a half hour."

Mera nodded, then opened the refrigerator, grabbed an apple, and left the room. The eyes of the women in the paintings followed her as she hurried to the front door.

Get a grip, she scolded herself, walking outside onto the porch. The morning was cool compared to those in Arizona, but the Maine air was heavy with humidity. The breeze from the ocean was a pleasant relief, slicing underneath the heaviness in swift, cool currents.

Salt water and grass mingled in the air. She noticed that sensation in the pit of her stomach again. That stirring in her core had never stopped, she realized, but had drifted to the back of her consciousness.

As Mera moved further away from the house, the yard became overgrown and untended, so unlike the interior of Ida's home. Mera marveled at the vibrant colors of the uncut grass, the wildflowers, the vines, and the heavy limbed trees where the forest met the edge of the lawn, breathing it all in as she walked. She took a worn path leading from the manicured lawn in front of the porch into the tall grass. It meandered along a slight curve out to the face of the cliff. Mera wondered with a sudden pang if her mother's feet had helped to carve the path on which she now walked.

At the end of the path, overlooking the cliff, Mera found a scene from a storybook: two willow trees, their branches forming a wispy green curtain that framed a stone bench sitting between them. Mera took a seat, leaning forward to see where the water met the cliffs. The waves were lapping against the rocks, dark green and slimy with moss and seaweed. She leaned back and closed her eyes, taking deep breaths of the clean salt air.

She had never seen the ocean before. Her mother had always been peculiar about the topic. Mera remembered a time a few years earlier when she was hanging out on the couch with her mother. They were each absorbed in their own novel, listening to one of her mom's records, a punk band's song about hitching a ride to the beach.

"We should take a trip to the beach someday," Mera thought out loud.

"No," her mom snapped, looking up from her book.

Mera laughed at first, but her mother's expression was serious.

"What do you mean, no?"

"Just what I said. No," her mother repeated.

They argued, and Mera stomped off to her bedroom, thinking even as she slammed the door how weird the argument was. But that was her mother—immovable about the strangest things. She never played that record again.

Listening to the waves splash against the rocks below, Mera wondered how many of her mother's curiosities she might discover the root of here.

The stirring in Mera's core jerked, and she dropped her apple. She gripped the edge of the stone bench with white knuckles, leaning forward to brace herself. Her gaze moved to the sea below where a dark patch was forming, as though ink had spilled and was now spreading. As the shape grew bigger and darkened to a jet black, a heaviness tightened around

Mera's heart. She clutched the bench even harder and tried to draw breath.

The wind picked up around her now, blowing hot and cold at once. Her eyes watered, and she struggled to stand. She could see the darkness in the water expanding, the outer edges snaking ever closer to the rocks below her.

The heaviness in her chest spread to her limbs. She took an involuntary step toward the edge of the cliff. She could see only the dark spot, its black surface glittering in the morning sun. It was right below her now.

Enough! a voice commanded, crystal clear in her mind, and the heaviness lifted. Mera turned away from the edge of the cliff and fell to her knees, drawing in rattling breaths. She blinked through her tears and looked again at the ocean. The dark patch in the water had disappeared. The waves had returned to normal.

"What are you doing out here?" Ida demanded, snapping Mera back to reality.

Mera jumped and turned. Ida was standing just behind the stone bench, those intense blue eyes boring into Mera's.

"I was just . . ." Mera started and then faltered under Ida's glare. She thought how to best explain the evil ocean inkblot to her grandmother. "I was, uh, just sitting."

"You do not come out here to sit or otherwise," Ida balked. "Is that understood?"

Mera bristled. "You're telling me I can't go outside?"

Ida gave her a withering glare. "You shouldn't be this close to the cliffs. It isn't safe."

For a brief second, Mera could see hints of her mother's face in Ida's. When she saw Mera studying her, Ida spun and stalked back up the path toward the house.

Mera didn't know what she had seen in the waves below, but it made her want to stay away from this spot from then on. On that point, at least, she and Ida agreed.

"Let's go!" Ida called through the overgrowth.

With gritted teeth, Mera walked the path back to the house and found her grandmother standing on the porch steps, waiting for her.

"Here," Ida said, thrusting something toward Mera.

Ida held out a glimmering silver chain with a small sea glass charm in the shape of a droplet of water. Mera held out her hand, and Ida placed the necklace in it. As soon as it hit her palm, a warmth emanated from the charm, tickling her fingertips and spreading over her hands. She loved it immediately—it felt like hers.

"It was Genevieve's," Ida explained, "Your mother's, I mean. I thought you'd want to have it."

Mera looked up at her grandmother and a shudder went through her. She remembered her dream—Ida's hands, working over something she couldn't make out through the glow.

It wasn't real, she reminded herself for the millionth time that morning. She slipped the necklace into her pocket.

"Thank you," Mera said.

Ida opened her mouth as if to say something but stopped. She rocked back on her heels and said, "We leave for school in five minutes. Meet me at the car." She disappeared back into the house.

***

Mera didn't know much about cars, but she knew Ida's was

ancient. It was an antique SUV that smelled of motor oil. It had faded paint on the outside and frayed seats. Mera assumed it had sentimental value to her grandmother (why else hold on to such a hunk of junk when Ida seemed to have the means to upgrade?). But as Ida shifted into gear, she muttered a steady stream of curse words under her breath until the car lurched forward, and they started down the long drive to the road.

At the middle of the driveway, Ida got out and unlocked and opened the gate. She got back in, drove through the posts, stopped, got back out, dragged it closed, and relocked it. The level of security seemed a little much to Mera. Had Ida forced Mera's mom to grow up like a member of a witness protection program, too?

They turned out of the driveway and passed through a stretch of dense forest before the greenery thinned and the ocean appeared through the trees on their left. Ida turned right, and they ascended a large hill, with a cluster of homes built closely together appearing at the crest. Mera realized it was the first set of houses she had seen since they left Ida's isolated driveway. On the other side of the hill, they passed more streets with houses built in proximity, then drove several miles before coming upon another set of streets and collection of houses. Mera wondered how many people lived here.

"Convergence is a village, in terms of population," Ida answered the question Mera had only thought. "We share the high school with Billings, our larger neighbor."

They reached what Mera assumed to be the village square. The streets narrowed but were more populated, filled with people bustling about their morning routines. They passed a laundromat, a diner, a meeting house with a plaque affixed next to its door that read 1774, and a few small shops.

Mera noticed Ida gripping the steering wheel with white knuckles. They stopped before a crosswalk where a woman pushing a baby carriage stepped out to cross. When she spotted the car, she squinted into it, staring at Ida and Mera until her baby let out a cry. She hurried away, pulling the carriage top over the baby.

Moments later, they slowed to a stop at a red light. An old couple on the corner gawked at them before leaning toward the passenger window so that their noses almost touched the glass. Mera looked at Ida, but she was staring straight ahead. Mera dropped lower in her seat as the light turned green.

Either the people in Convergence were nosy, or her grandmother was noteworthy.

They passed through another patch of woods, and on the other side of the woods, they pulled up across the street from Billings High School and parked. Mera saw hordes of teenagers streaming toward the entrance. The school was massive, taking up the entire block, and made of bright red brick with a white stone entryway that peaked in a series of three pointed arches. Mera watched a few students get swallowed up in the entrance's shadow as they passed through before she realized Ida was staring at her hands.

"You don't have to wear it. But it's valuable, so don't lose it."

Mera wasn't sure when she had pulled the necklace out of her pocket, but she grasped it in her clenched fist. The corners of the droplet charm pressed hard into her skin, and she relaxed her hand. She shoved the necklace back into her pocket and reached for her backpack.

"Go straight to the office; they're expecting you," Ida instructed, the steel edge back in her voice. "As soon as school is over, I will wait here to pick you up. Come right out."

Mera nodded. She got out of the car, then leaned back in. "Uh, bye," she said.

Ida was gripping the steering wheel and staring straight ahead, avoiding Mera like she had the people in the town. "Yes. Goodbye."

Mera closed the door. As she walked toward the school entrance, the necklace grew warm against her leg through her pocket's thin cotton, warmer than it should be from regular friction. Mera shook off the thought. A heat-retaining family heirloom was the least of her concerns. Heads turned after her as she hurried up the steps to the main entrance.

She tried her best to keep her head down before disappearing through the door.

FOUR

IN THE FRONT office, Mera approached the desk of an older woman sitting behind a nameplate reading Mrs. Midge. Her desk was neat but busy, a row of trinkets lining the edge. On the center of her desk, lying open, was a folder with Mera's name written in black ink across the top. Mrs. Midge looked up as Mera approached, peering at her from behind red square glasses.

"And how can I help you this morning?" Mrs. Midge chirped.

"I'm here to . . . register, I guess?" Mera said.

"Mera, then, is it? Did you hear that, Mrs. Tolland?" Mrs. Midge called to the woman filing papers into mailbox slots. "Mera *Kellen* is here to register."

"What?" Mrs. Tolland called over her shoulder.

"Ida's granddaughter," Mrs. Midge replied, "is here to *register.*"

This time, Mrs. Tolland spun around so fast that one envelope in her hand followed her spin trajectory and sailed across the room, hitting an empty trash can with a loud metallic thud.

"Marie!" Mrs. Midge chided Mrs. Tolland, turning back to Mera. "Sorry, we don't hear much from the Kellens these days! How long will you be with us, dear?"

Mera looked down to avoid the woman's buggy gaze and saw that the first page in her folder was her schedule. She glanced over and saw Mrs. Tolland was still staring at her, unmoved from her spot at the mailboxes. She had to leave before Mrs. Midge alerted more of her colleagues to her lineage.

"Is that mine?" Mera said as she snatched the printed schedule from the folder. "Great! Thanks a million!" She was out the door before the receptionists had finished sputtering.

Mera waded into the crowd of students. Based on what she had seen so far this morning, to call Ida a social outcast would be generous. What could Ida have done?

Mera found the door emblazoned with the number of her first class. She walked into the classroom, humming with students, and she made a beeline for the teacher's desk. A low buzz picked up as a handful of kids bowed their heads in small groups and looked back up at her.

"Hi, I'm—" Mera began when she reached the desk.

"Mera Kellen! Of course, welcome!" the teacher chirped, a square-shaped woman with oversized glasses. "I'm Ms. Powell."

Mera smiled, then shot a furtive glance over her shoulder at her new, gawking classmates.

"You'll have to excuse us. We don't have that many new faces in Convergence. You can take a seat in the back left there next to Ani. She's in the blue shirt," Ms. Powell said.

She handed Mera her calculus textbook as the warning bell

rang, and then she bustled off to set up for the day's lesson. Mera lowered her head and made her way through the throng of curious faces. She found the girl Ms. Powell had called Ani. Ani was wearing a light blue shirt and a long, floral skirt with bright pink sneakers poking out underneath it. She had her calculus textbook propped up in front of her, her wide eyes unblinkingly scanning the page.

As Mera dropped into the empty desk beside her, Mera gave her a weak smile when their eyes met over the brim of the book. Ani sank lower in her seat, shrinking her slight frame even more. Her black, bobbed hair fell over her face like a curtain, hiding her from view.

The last bell rang, and Ms. Powell began the lesson, still fidgeting with the projector as she spoke.

"Good morning, mathematicians!" she called in a sing-song voice, slapping the side of the projector. "We're welcoming a new student today, who I know will become *integral* to our class "

Ms. Powell laughed and looked around at the students staring back at her. Mera saw Ani shake her head sympathetically out of the corner of her eye.

"Anyway, everyone please welcome Mera Kellen," Ms. Powell said, resigned.

Heads turned Mera's way as more whispers broke out around the room. Mera felt her face turn scarlet. Two girls in the row in front of Mera looked at Mera and Ani with feigned delight.

"Aww, isn't that so cute," the first girl said.

"The phantom made a friend," the second girl replied.

Ani lowered the textbook and glowered at them as Ms.

Powell called everyone's attention back to the front.

Mera locked eyes with one of them, and her smirk faltered. Mera swore she saw a flicker of fear go through her before she dropped her gaze and turned around. The other girl threw one last contemptuous look at Ani and faced forward.

Mera looked over at Ani, who hid behind her textbook again.

Make new friends, Mera thought to herself as she sighed and flipped open her new textbook. *Check.*

***

A few hours later, Mera walked into the cafeteria for lunch. This wasn't her first time navigating a new high school lunch minefield, having moved often with her mother. Her morning was so strange, she wasn't sure her usual "blend into the wall" strategy would work here.

Most of the student body at Billings High regarded her with passing interest, but there were several students in her morning classes who, like the ones in calculus, stared at her with fascination or contempt. It didn't help that Ani peered at her from behind her textbook throughout all of their shared classes when she thought Mera wasn't looking.

Mera moved through the lunch line and sat at the opposite end of a table with a few kids she recognized from her English class. She exchanged a polite smile with the group but kept to her own side, not wanting to impose on any existing social arrangements. A familiar prickle on the back of her neck made Mera turn to see Ani a few tables behind her, staring at something just over Mera's head. *Of course*, Mera thought, shaking her head and turning back around.

Mera was finishing her lunch when a loud bark of laughter

from the cafeteria entrance made her look up. Students scurried out of the way of a group of kids (the word *pack* jumped to Mera's mind) entering the lunchroom. There were six of them—three boys, three girls—and their very presence made others jump out of their path.

There was something oddly similar about the group members, from their dark brown hair to their perfectly structured faces to their square builds. Dressed in a style that Mera could only describe as "preppy," they wore collared shirts, sweaters, khaki pants, and pleated skirts. Mera glanced at her own clothes. Her mom and she prided themselves on being thrift store experts, but Mera's faded jeans and worn flannel seemed lackluster in current company.

Another chorus of yipping laughter made Mera lift her head again. The boys were busy jostling each other as the girls rolled their eyes but giggled. It was as though they were auditioning for their own teenage sitcom, of which they were the stars, and the rest of the school was their audience. Mera noticed that everyone in the cafeteria was keeping one eye on them, even the teachers on lunch duty.

One girl stepped out in front of the pack. Her hair was stick-straight, not a strand out of place. She walked with impeccable posture—her head held so high, Mera wondered how she could even see where she was going. The rest of her friends fell into step behind her. She was approaching one table with a wide smile, exposing rows of perfect teeth.

"Wyatt!" she called, her voice high-pitched, yet strong enough to carry across the cafeteria.

"Hey, Tara," replied the boy who must've been Wyatt. He had been alone before the group approached and appeared to be an unwilling host. Wyatt had blackish-brown hair (wavy, yet tousled, Mera noticed) and was decidedly different from the pack now falling into the seats next to him. He was a much simpler dresser, for one—wearing a T-shirt and jeans versus the preppy-pack's coordinated outfits. But it was something else. He was *warmer*.

Mera was so absorbed in studying Wyatt that she hadn't noticed the cafeteria go silent. She looked away from Wyatt and locked eyes with Tara, who was staring at her hard. The necklace in Mera's jeans pocket burned, and she let out an involuntary gasp, clutching her leg.

The pack erupted in laughter, except for Tara. She smirked and stood, moving toward Mera without taking her eyes off her. An oncoming student had to dive out of her way, sending his tray clattering to the ground. Mera thought she heard the kid mutter an apology before retreating to a nearby table for cover.

After another scan of the cafeteria, Mera realized everyone was staring at them. She peeked at the kids from her English class, who had retreated so far down the bench they were in danger of falling off. With a tinge of annoyance, Mera turned back to face Tara.

With Tara's approach, the necklace grew warmer in Mera's pocket. The surrounding air went still.

"Mera Kellen," Tara said, stopping in front of Mera. Tara tossed her hair as she looked at her friends. They exchanged excited looks. Mera realized she could sense their anticipation building. Anticipation and something else . . . anger.

It was rolling off Tara as she faced Mera, her top lip raised in a sneer. The stillness in the air grew more uncomfortable by the second.

"Yup, that's me," Mera said. "Is yelling out people's names in the cafeteria a hobby of yours? If I knew yours, maybe I could join in the fun."

Mera glanced at Wyatt, who was staring back and forth between Mera and Tara with growing concern. She looked back up at Tara. The smirk vanished from her face, replaced by a cold fury. The air constricted around Mera, and her necklace sent another blast of heat through her pant leg.

"Oh, don't worry," Tara smirked again. "You'll find out."

She turned on her heel. Her friends followed, cackling and shooting menacing glances over their shoulders at Mera. The air returned to normal, and her necklace cooled. The noise in the cafeteria raised to its regular volume (although Mera suspected the sudden chatter was likely about what had just happened).

Only when the pack dispersed did she notice Wyatt walking in her direction, carrying his lunch tray. As he passed, Wyatt flashed Mera a quick smile that reached his eyes, which were a luminous yellow-brown. Mera felt as though she were standing in the sun after being in a cold room for too long. Wyatt continued past her and the sensation vanished. He crossed the cafeteria to clear his tray and exit in the opposite direction of Tara and her lackeys.

Mera wasn't sure what confused her more—that she already had enemies, that her necklace was heating at random intervals, or that the air shifted based on who was closest to her.

She searched for her wide-eyed admirer, but Ani was nowhere in sight. Mera was alone.

***

Whatever the pack's reasoning for marking Mera an undesirable, the effects were immediate. After lunch, no one spoke to her except her teachers, and even some of them treated her with an icy indifference.

When the bell rang at the end of the day, Mera let the other students jostle through the classroom door while she waited for the hallways to clear. After studying the map of the school on the back of her schedule, she took the longer path to the front entrance, through the locker-less library wing. It would allow her to avoid the bustle of the remaining students and save them the trouble of having to pretend she was invisible.

The library wing was a dark hallway with low ceilings and dim overhead lights, but the end of the hall opened into a bright glass atrium. Connecting the library wing to the main entrance, the atrium was bathed in afternoon light. As Mera crossed into the atrium, she stopped short and closed her eyes, turning her face toward the sky. The warmth washed over her in the first quiet moment she'd had all day. It reminded her of the necklace in her pocket, which had remained dormant since lunch. She pulled it out and held it in her hand, rubbing her thumb over the small glass charm.

Eyes closed, she sensed they were there before the necklace flashed warm, the air restricting around her. Mera opened her eyes and saw her fan club from the cafeteria blocking her path to the main entrance.

"So, is this like, a bullying thing, or what?"

They glowered at her in silence. Tara took a step closer to her.

"A Kellen being bullied," Tara let out a humorless chuckle

that reverberated around the atrium. "In Convergence, we call it retribution."

There it was again, this obsession with her family name. It didn't occur to them that, despite a shared last name, Ida was as much of a stranger to Mera as they were.

There was no mistaking Tara was trembling with rage. What was going on? And why hadn't Ida warned her?

"Well, I'm sorry to interrupt your little vengeance plot, or whatever, but I was just leaving," Mera said, gesturing to the group blocking her path, the necklace in her open palm.

Tara's eyes narrowed on the charm. She took a step toward Mera, who instinctively stepped backward, closing her fist around the necklace. The sea glass charm was unbearably hot now.

"I guess we can add dirty thieves to the Kellen family crest," Tara spat. "Where did you get that?"

The air thickened, like it was hardening around her. Mera drew in a more labored breath, trying to keep her composure.

"Why do you care?" Mera asked.

"Because it doesn't belong to you," Tara snarled. "But that's par for the course with your family, isn't it? Taking things you have no right to?"

Mera pushed the necklace into her pocket, too hot for her to hold any longer. "I don't know what you're babbling about. I still don't even know who you are."

"There isn't enough time in the day to explain all the things you don't know," Tara said with another mirthless laugh, balling her hands into fists at her side. An invisible molasses filled up the room, rooting Mera in place. She had a fleeting thought of bugs frozen in amber. "But let's start with one of the obvious ones, shall we? Where is your traitor mother, anyway, Kellen?"

At the mention of her mother, anger crashed over Mera like a tidal wave. The heat from the charm in her pocket imploded, flooding her body with a coursing hot spring that snaked up her abdomen and buoyed her heart. It traveled through the muscles in her arms, pushing out into her fingertips, forcing her hands to tense and stretch at her side. The molasses melted away around her.

Then, an inexplicable lightness cut through the air, though Mera could see nothing. In the next moment, Tara and her friends toppled over like bowling pins. Tara scurried to her feet first, groping at the surrounding air, spinning on the spot.

"*Airhead!*" she screamed, her voice muffled in the heavy air filling the glass atrium, her eyes still wildly searching as she brushed dirt off her outfit.

From the wall on the far side of the atrium came the distinctive click of the fire alarm handle, followed by its ear-splitting shriek.

Tara ran out of the room, cursing. Her friends scrambled off the ground and followed in a panic. Mera stood staring at the pulled fire alarm, with no one in sight.

Dazed, Mera walked across the atrium to the now blinking alarm, as if inspecting it closer would produce some explanation.

"Young *lady!*" a gruff voice exclaimed.

The lightness in the air brushed by Mera, the whisper of a giggle echoing up to the glass ceiling.

FIVE

PRINCIPAL CROWLEY WAS staring across his desk at Mera, disbelief creasing his features. He was a tall, solid man, with a boxy upper body and a thick neck that gathered at his starched collar. They hadn't spoken on the quick march to his office, and he had left her alone for some time as he sorted out everything with the local firefighters when they arrived. Mera's ears were still ringing from the blaring of the alarm as she stared back at him now, waiting for her punishment to begin.

"Well," he began with a huff.

He picked up a stack of papers on his desk and reshuffled them, making small noises of incredulity. He gestured as if he expected her to speak, but she didn't know what to say. How could she defend herself? The "invisible, giggling wind pulled the fire alarm" defense wasn't likely to earn her any points with her new principal, so she said nothing. He tossed the stack of papers down with a great sigh, scattering them again.

"Now I understand it has been . . ." he began, folding his hands and leaning closer to her, attempting to soften his voice, ". . . a tough time for you, Ms. Kellen. But what message are you sending with this behavior, on your first day, no less," he finished in an impatient hiss.

When Mera said nothing, he let out another huff and sat back. "I don't know what your personal issues are, but we will not give you preferential treatment no matter the . . . family situation."

Principal Crowley looked up past Mera and waved someone into the office before she could respond. Mera turned to see a slight, middle-aged woman, about the same age as her mom, with unnaturally blonde hair enter the room. She gave Mera a small smile as she sat next to her and then faced Principal Crowley.

"With that being said, this is Ms. Hughes, the guidance counselor," Principal Crowley said, seeming to re-inflate at the prospect of passing the problem of Mera to someone else. "Starting tomorrow, you will meet with her to discuss your —"

"Personal issues," Mera offered.

"Yes, personal issues," Principal Crowley said, and then paused, looking at Mera again. "Ms. Hughes is our best line of defense against . . ." He trailed off again, holding up his hands, as if whatever Mera had to discuss with Ms. Hughes was beyond anything he could understand.

"Hello, Mera," Ms. Hughes said in a quiet tone. "I look forward to speaking with you." The necklace twitched in Mera's pocket.

There was a loud clatter in the doorway. Mera turned to find Ida there, her face drawn more than Mera had ever seen it. Mrs. Midge and Mrs. Tolland were visible just over her shoulder, watching the scene with wide, almost starstruck eyes. Principal Crowley's face had turned white, while Ms. Hughes's smirk faltered.

"What is this?" Ida demanded, her eyes darting around the office.

"Hello, Ida," Ms. Hughes said, sounding like she was suppressing the smallest laugh.

Ida fixed her glare on Ms. Hughes for a long, silent moment before turning to address Principal Crowley.

"What," Ida repeated, her voice controlled but permeating anger, "is this?"

"Ida, please," Principal Crowley murmured, "we would have called to inform you sooner, but—" he paused, looking at Ms. Hughes and then Mera. "We should speak in private."

Moments later, Mera was sitting outside the closed office door, trying in vain to listen to the conversation that followed. There was a scraping of chairs, and Ida strode out of the office. Mera stood to follow Ida, glancing into the open door of the office. Principal Crowley (who was so pale he appeared almost green) and Ms. Hughes had their heads bowed in whispered conversation. Ms. Hughes looked up at Mera as she passed, that same hidden smile on her face.

Mera hurried out of the building after her grandmother.

The drive back to Ida's house was silent. Principal Crowley must have told Ida that Mera had set off the fire alarm. As she watched the trees thicken as they moved further away from the center of town, Mera was too distracted to care what any of them thought she had or hadn't done, anyway. Even if she tried to explain, what would she say?

The vivid dreams. That pulling deep in her core. The dark

churning in the ocean drawing her to the edge. The air and the way it changed around Tara, her cronies, and the boy with the tousled hair. Invisible forces pulling a fire alarm. And most distressing, that tidal wave of heat that had taken her over. An energized current pumping through her veins in rhythm to the throbbing of the necklace in her pocket, even now.

Mera pressed her forehead against the car window, lost in thought. Before she arrived at her grandmother's house, she had experienced strange occurrences. A light pull on her navel as she submerged herself in the bath, or a spike in heat in the air when she was upset or angry. She could sometimes anticipate what people were going to say or do or convince people to change their minds or tell her things. She used to chalk these incidents up to her imagination, or an uncanny skill at reading people. But even her best excuses didn't help explain the mystifying episodes her mother used to have.

It could happen any time—sitting together on the couch, walking through the park. Mera's mother would clutch at her heart, her eyes clenched shut, her body wracked with tremors that often spread to the surrounding ground. When it was over, and the floor stopped shaking, Mera's mother explained it away. A panic attack, or low blood sugar. But Mera had never met another person for whom anxiety or a late lunch caused small seismic events.

Then there was that night three months ago. Mera's mother had gone to bed early, her face flushed, complaining of a headache. As Mera finished her homework at the kitchen table, she heard what sounded like an explosion from her mother's bedroom. Mera found all the glass in the room shattered. Her mother sat up in bed, tiny cuts from the glass shards covering her face and hands. She looked at Mera, and for a moment, Mera didn't recognize the person looking back at her, her eyes stormy pools of glowing light. Then she blinked, and her eyes returned to their familiar shade of sapphire. The next day, with both of Genevieve's hands bandaged, they moved again. This time to Phoenix.

Mera's mother never spoke of these events, and Mera was too afraid to ask. A part of her knew that her mother's primary motivation for keeping Mera in the dark was to protect her. But, Mera realized with a pit in her stomach, there had been no one to protect Genevieve.

Before Mera knew it, they were pulling into Ida's driveway. She watched as Ida undid the gate halfway up the drive and the pit in her stomach tightened. What was with her grandmother and this compound? What was Ida protecting herself from? Did it have anything to do with the shadows that haunted her mother?

Mera had to understand her "family situation" if she was going to find her mother. And she was sure Ida—secretive, suspicious, and uncooperative—had to be the skeleton key to unlocking the mystery.

They parked, and Mera followed Ida inside and into the sitting room. It had formal couches and stiff-backed chairs arranged in the center of the room, with another large mural of the sun carved into a wooden panel above the fireplace. Ida motioned for Mera to take a seat on the firm, burgundy velvet couch, which she did. Ida sat opposite her and stared at Mera.

"You had an eventful first day of school," Ida said, her voice even. She clasped her hands in her lap.

"You could say that," Mera replied. "Turns out, our family

is very popular."

She wanted to see what Ida would give away, but her grandmother's face remained controlled.

"Oh?" Ida said.

"Did you not think to mention that you're a local legend?" Mera said, her annoyance flaring. "I spent my entire day feeling like I was in a zoo exhibit."

"Ah, so you pulled the fire alarm to . . . divert attention," Ida said.

"Maybe popular isn't the right word," Mera said, tapping her chin in mock consideration.

"No? Then how would you describe it? Now that you've drawn the attention of the principal, the local fire department, and the Hughes woman?"

"Must be genetic, since the sight of you makes half the town gawk and the other half run away."

"Let me ask you again. What happened at school today?"

A tingle at the base of Mera's skull trickled down her spine, but she didn't look away. How was Mera supposed to trust Ida to believe the truth, when Ida didn't trust Mera at all? With a fresh pang of sadness, Mera missed her mom, who had believed her always and without reservation.

"Some kids dared me to pull the alarm," Mera lied, pushing her sadness away and letting stubbornness take its place. "You know, a little light hazing. No big, won't happen again."

Ida narrowed her eyes at Mera then asked again. "What happened at school, Mera?"

Ida's voice was thick with more than just authority—it had a low growl of power. The tingle turned into a shiver as the question went through her. Images flashed through her mind

—the empty library hallway, the teenagers in the atrium, the charge of the charm in her pocket, her hands stretching, tingling at her sides. Before she knew what she was doing, Mera forced the lie to her mind, and the images changed. She saw herself standing at the fire alarm, her hand on the handle, the blare of the alarm in her ears.

Her mind cleared, and she and Ida were staring at one another. Though Ida was just over the coffee table, she felt very far away.

"Teenagers," Mera said, shrugging.

Ida stood from the couch, a cloud over her features.

"Go to your room. Now," she breathed.

Mera stood and left the room. She chanced one last look at Ida as she ran upstairs. Her grandmother stared at the spot where Mera had been sitting, a troubled expression on her face.

SIX

MERA AWOKE THE next morning feeling like she had only just closed her eyes, her alarm blaring. She dressed for school in a daze and was standing with her hand on her bedroom door when she stopped. She reached into her hamper, shaking the necklace out of her jeans from the day before. The charm was cool in her hand, its weight reassuring. She held it up and let the sunlight filtering in through her bedroom window catch the droplet in its rays, casting the silver-threaded walls in rainbows. It was clear to Mera why she loved the necklace, but she still didn't understand what Tara wanted with it.

Mera clasped the necklace around her neck and tucked the charm beneath her T-shirt, hoping the lack of friction from her jeans would keep it from overheating like it had the day before. It sat lightly on her chest, a cool, smooth, undetectable droplet. It was her mother's, Mera sensed that, and her mother was someone Mera needed a connection with now more than ever.

***

After a terse car ride with Ida, Mera also received the silent treatment at school. The only time people looked directly at her was when they navigated around her in the hallway. Tara and her friends' influence at the school impressed Mera even if she didn't understand it.

Ani's seat was empty for most of the period, but she came in brandishing a late pass as Ms. Powell was dividing them into partners to share their answers.

"Oh, perfect!" Ms. Powell said, taking Ani's pass. "Now you can partner up with Mera."

Ani looked stricken, and a few kids snickered. Mera's cheeks flushed red as Ani made her way to her seat and everyone got started on their assignment. Mera shifted her desk to face her unwilling partner, and Ani sat with her backpack still on, sitting rigid and uncomfortable in her seat, averting her eyes from Mera.

"Do you need a minute to catch up?" Mera asked. "Or . . . something?"

"Um, nope, all caught up," Ani said, shaking her head and shrugging. "No catching up needed."

"You know what the assignment is, even though you weren't here and didn't do it?" Mera asked, incredulous, as Ani stared transfixed by the wood grain on her desk.

"Right. No. Okay, bring on the catching up," Ani admitted, looking embarrassed. She pulled her backpack out from around her and took out a pencil and her notebook. The cover was light blue and covered in doodles. They reminded Mera of the etchings on Ida's dining-room windows, of delicate people riding the wind.

Mera looked at Ani, their eyes meeting for the first time. Mera felt a tingle at the top of her spine, and an image flashed in her mind. It was the scene from the atrium the day before, but from a different point of view. Mera watched herself advancing toward the pulled fire alarm as Tara and her friends scattered.

Mera blinked, and the image disappeared.

"Wait," Mera sputtered, piecing together what she had seen. "It was you?"

Ani's large brown eyes were wide and glittering with . . . was that excitement?

"I knew it!" Ani cried, banging her small fist on the desk. She let out a yip of laughter, and the girls in the row in front of them turned and rolled their eyes.

"Wait, what did I see?" Mera asked, her mind racing. "You're the one who pulled the fire alarm?"

Ani looked at Mera like she had forgotten she was there.

"Not here," she whispered, unable to hide her smile. "I'll find you after school."

"What? No!" Mera sputtered. "Tell me what's going on."

The bell rang, and the room erupted in noise as chairs scraped across the linoleum, Ms. Powell yelled half-heard instructions, and the students raced for the door. Ani hopped out of her seat.

"I'll find you, I promise!" she said, vanishing into the stream of students.

***

Two hours later, Mera still could not shake what she had seen or put her finger on how she had seen it. She found herself so lost in thought, it took her a moment to register her English teacher repeating her name.

"Mera?" Mr. Diaz was saying, the classroom phone to his ear. "You're wanted in Ms. Hughes's office."

Mera had forgotten her sentence of counseling doled out by Principal Crowley. She collected her belongings, the stares of her classmates following her out the classroom door.

At the counselor's office, Mera found the door open. Ms. Hughes was at her desk, closing a folder. She looked up and smiled at Mera.

"Mera, hello!" she said, gesturing to the chair in front of her desk. "Please, come in."

Mera sat and assessed the office. It was tidy but sterile. Large steel filing cabinets covered most of the far wall as well as a couple sparsely adorned bookshelves. Mera noted a lack of motivational posters encouraging her to reach for the stars, and even Ms. Hughes's desk had only a few essential items— a nameplate, a phone, and the single folder that Mera assumed had her name printed across the top.

Ms. Hughes stood and crossed the room to close the door. Despite Ms. Hughes's soft demeanor, she had a hurried gait.

"Now, since this is our first meeting," Ms. Hughes started as she settled across from Mera, "we'll be getting acquainted with one another. How is your second day going?"

"Fine," Mera said.

Ms. Hughes smiled again and folded her hands atop the desk. Her fingers were long and spindly, and although her fingernails were a sleek shade of olive green, the skin on her hands looked rough and weathered.

"Lovely," she sighed, "simply lovely to hear."

Mera raised her eyebrows and nodded, looking around the room again. Out of the corner of her eye, she saw Ms. Hughes never took her focus off her.

"I want you to feel comfortable here, Mera. One's

environment must be conducive to growth."

"I am, like, so comfortable, thank you," Mera replied, every muscle in her body clenched.

"Mera, I understand. You've been through a lot recently. Your mother, gone. Sent to live with a . . . stranger. I mean, your grandmother is hardly the most agreeable person," Ms. Hughes said with a soft laugh.

Mera got the sense Ms. Hughes and Ida knew each other, but how well? Mera tried to keep her expression neutral but pursed her lips despite herself.

"I'm not trying to pry, of course, I noticed yesterday that things between you seemed a little . . . tense, shall we say? I am simply here as a resource, and a friend. If you are experiencing anything strange—anything that feels scary, or that you don't understand—I'm here to help you through it. That's all."

Mera resisted the urge to shift in her seat. Ms. Hughes was speaking generally, of course. She had to be. There was no way for Ms. Hughes to realize how specifically her advice applied to the last forty-eight hours of Mera's life. Right?

"All I'm saying is that none of this can be easy. And please forgive me if I'm out of line, but Ida Kellen isn't known for making things easier," she said conspiratorially, that familiar smirk playing at the corners of her mouth.

Not trusting herself to respond, Mera said nothing. Ms. Hughes looked at her for a long minute and let out another soft sigh.

"I realize I might be saying things that you aren't quite ready to say yourself. Here, in this space," Ms. Hughes gestured around at her barren office, "you are completely safe. And I will be here to listen whenever you're ready to express yourself, or discuss any of the new . . . experiences you might be having."

After another stretched-out silence, all Mera could think to say was, "Super."

"Okay then," Ms. Hughes replied. She pulled a scrap of paper and a pen from the top drawer of her desk and scribbled a pass to return Mera to class.

"You know," she said, signing her name in an elegant flourish, "it's not like there's any rush. We have the whole year to open you up."

She smiled wide this time, baring her white teeth, receding in a perfect row under her thin lips. They were smooth like identical pearls.

"Well, Mera," Ms. Hughes said in response to Mera's silence. "It's been a pleasure getting acquainted. I'll see you at the same time next week."

Ms. Hughes held out the pass to her, and Mera leaned forward to take it, ready to be out of her office, but Ms. Hughes pulled it back again.

"One last thing, Mera. I just want to say how sorry I am about your mother."

Mera's heart beat hard in her chest, but she said nothing.

"I was so hoping she would overcome her . . . past here," Ms. Hughes said, shaking her head. "But it appears Ida won after all."

Mera stared at her. Her mother's past? What did she need to overcome? What did Ida win? Ms. Hughes seemed to be about her mother's age. Did she know her mother? Mera felt a twinge around her neckline under her sweater as the necklace thumped in rhythm with her heartbeat. The sly smile returned to Ms. Hughes's face.

"Now let's get you back to class before the lunch bell rings!" Ms. Hughes said, leaning forward to give Mera the piece of paper.

As Mera reached for the pass, Ms. Hughes's fingers brush her own. The necklace around her throat emitted a sudden jolt, sending a shock through her body and down her fingertips. Ms. Hughes's hand flew back, slamming hard onto the desk. She yelped in pain, grabbing her hand and staring at Mera with a sudden cold intensity, all hints of a smile gone.

Mera realized she had the pass clenched so tightly, it was crumbling in her fingers.

"Must have been static," Mera blurted out.

"You pack quite a punch, don't you?" Ms. Hughes breathed, her smirk crinkling the corners of her eyes as she peered at Mera. She was still cradling her hand.

"Sorry," Mera said just before she bolted.

She emerged in the hallway as the bell rang for lunch, and she threw herself into the crush of students. Determined to avoid another confrontation with Tara and the gang, she steered clear of the cafeteria. Mera darted into a deserted hallway lined with display cabinets. She walked until the noise from the busy hallways dissipated. Mera leaned against the wall between two trophy cases and slid to the floor, exhausted.

Her heart was still racing, her skin prickling. She pulled the necklace out from under her shirt and unclasped it from around her neck, holding it in her palm to inspect. Mera was sure the shock in Ms. Hughes's office originated from the necklace, though that wasn't possible.

She stared at it for a few more moments, turning it over in her hands, before blinking back tears and refastening it around her neck. Ms. Hughes's comment about her mother seemed pointed. She didn't trust Ms. Hughes or her smirk—she wouldn't be surprised if she was just goading Mera into providing her with fodder about Ida for the town gossip mill. But Ms. Hughes wanted her to know that there was a town consensus about her grandmother, and that Mera should be equally distrustful of Ida.

Mera wondered why everyone was familiar with her grandmother, though Ida kept to herself and out of the public eye, holed up in her house. Lost in a haze of conspiratorial anxiety, Mera didn't notice him until he was dropping down next to her on the floor.

"That's some necklace," he said.

It was Wyatt, the boy from the cafeteria yesterday, with the wavy, tousled hair. He was half smiling at her, his brown eyes speckled golden yellow, kind and inquisitive. They reminded Mera of the charcoal sun drawing in Ida's dining room when it caught the sunlight. Her brain went fuzzy, and she shook her head, furrowing her brow in annoyance.

"So I've heard," Mera huffed.

Wyatt, smile unfaltering, held out his hand. "I'm Wyatt."

Mera hesitated, but unlike Ms. Hughes, his smile reached all the way to his eyes. "Mera," she held out her hand to shake his.

As he took her hand, a flash of indescribable tingling erupted up her arm, leaving goosebumps in its wake. The nerve endings from where their skin met fired like she was holding a lit firecracker, jolts of heat and electricity coursing through her.

It lasted only a second before Mera pulled her hand out of his. His eyes were wide, and he cradled his own hand to his chest and stared at it. Neither spoke for a moment. Mera's fingertips still tingled.

"So," Mera said shakily. "Does everyone in this town have intrusive opinions about accessories?"

Wyatt laughed. "Not that I know of. It's . . . a bold statement." He gestured at the necklace.

Mera looked down at it again, with its small, unassuming glass charm. What was so controversial about it?

"This?" she asked, holding up the charm. "A bold statement?"

"Well, yeah," Wyatt stammered. "I mean, in Convergence, at least."

"I wasn't aware Convergence was such a fashion capital," Mera quipped. She tucked the necklace back into her T-shirt.

Wyatt cocked his head to one side, studying her, as if he was unsure whether he should laugh. "Right. Fashion."

The air stirred around them. Warmth radiated from Wyatt like a space heater. Mera's heart quickened, and her muscles relaxed. She was reminded of that cozy sensation of being tucked under a thick blanket on a cold night.

The ringing of the bell sliced through Mera's reverie, signaling the end of the lunch period. They scrambled to their feet as students began trickling into the hallway.

Wyatt hesitated before holding out his hand again.

"Well, Mera, it was nice to meet you."

She, too, hesitated for a brief second, her stomach

fluttering with fear and excitement, before she slipped her hand into his. The effect was instantaneous—her blood turning to a rich lava where he touched her, coursing a velvet heat through her arm. They pulled their hands away, and Wyatt joined the crowd moving away from the cafeteria.

Mera felt the tingling sensation of his hand in hers, his fingers pressing their strange heat into her skin, the rest of the day.

SEVEN

MERA GATHERED HER belongings when the last bell rang, looking for Ani as she walked toward the school entrance. "I'll find you," Ani had said. Something told her she wouldn't find Ani until she wanted to be found.

"I'm glad retrieving you from the principal's office won't be a daily chore," Ida said by way of greeting as Mera climbed into the car a few minutes later.

"Well, there's always tomorrow," Mera said.

"So," Ida said, her hand on the car key in the ignition, eyes forward. "How was your day?"

Mera looked at Ida out of the corner of her eye.

"I met with Ms. Hughes," Mera said, not seeing the point of keeping it a secret.

Ida bristled, straightening up and starting the car. "That is unfortunate. I thought I made myself clear. I will have to speak to Principal Crowley again."

Mera turned to look at Ida. While she would take any excuse to get out of sitting across from Ms. Hughes, something more was going on.

"Unless, of course, you wish to have someone to speak

with," Ida said. "About . . . anything."

The concern in her grandmother's voice surprised Mera. But she couldn't shake her distrust of Ida. Not yet.

"No. She's weird."

"Always trust your instincts. They are the only truth you need."

"My mom used to say that."

She turned to her grandmother, who looked back at her with softened eyes, then turned back to the road.

They drove on deeper into the forest, the dense canopy throwing late afternoon shadows onto the pavement ahead of them like a monochrome kaleidoscope.

Ida tensed as the car crossed the boundary to the driveway from the road.

"What?" Mera asked.

"We have company."

As the car crept up the drive, Mera saw that the gate was wide open. Anger radiated from Ida—it made the hair on Mera's arms stand on end, and the necklace twinged hot against her chest.

They pulled in sight of the house to find a police car parked out front. On the porch stood an officer, his arms crossed. He turned and took his sunglasses off, stepping down from the porch as they parked.

Ida reached for the door handle then turned to Mera.

"Say nothing," she said and opened the door.

Mera scrambled to follow her out of the car, not wanting to miss any of her grandmother in action.

The police officer was a squat, bulwark of a man, all muscle and bulk. He had dark hair and deep-set eyes that reminded Mera of craters in a rock face. Ida towered over him by almost a head as they drew closer. There was something familiar about him. Then he smirked, and she realized who he must be.

"Ida," Tara's father said, his voice deep.

The necklace throbbed again, sending another current of energy into Mera's chest.

"Rochester," Ida replied, distaste etched on every feature of her face. Ida shifted to position herself in front of Mera, blocking her from view. Mera peered around her.

"*Sheriff* Rochester," the sheriff said, his smirk expanding. "I know you don't get out much anymore, but try to remember your manners."

"Ah, and how civil it was for you to let yourself onto my private property," Ida replied. "The gate on the driveway is locked for a reason."

"Locked?" he asked, feigning surprise. "You forgot to close it—it happens a lot with women your age. You'll want to be more careful."

Ida said nothing. In the silence that followed, a warm stream of air flowed steadily from Ida. Standing behind her was like standing next to an open oven. Mera took a step backward, putting her in full view of the sheriff, who stared at her hard. The necklace jumped.

"So, this must be Gennie's girl," Rochester glowered at her.

Mera had never heard anyone refer to her mother as Gennie before, but she knew her mom would hate it.

"So, little Gennie takes off without a word, and sixteen years later, this one shows up. Your family is full of surprises, huh?" Rochester gave a joyless laugh. "Did you even know this girl existed? Or did you find out a couple days ago, like the rest of us?"

Mera's heart hummed inside of her chest as Rochester's words reverberated in her brain. Could she have left Convergence to hide her pregnancy? It was a secret from the nosy people in town. That was understandable, but did she keep it from Ida, too?

"Do not speak about my family, Rochester."

"You don't want to talk about family? Then let's talk about respect," Rochester snapped. "How about respect for our community? I waited for you to do the right thing. To follow the rules. Bring the girl before the council and introduce her to the village. But of course, you never showed up. And with that fire alarm stunt yesterday, I had to come inspect her for myself."

The sheriff took a step toward Mera. The heat swelled around her grandmother, and Rochester stopped short.

"Ida, you can't afford any more trouble than you're already in," he said, his smirk spreading across his face like an infection.

Mera looked at Ida. Trouble? For taking in her own granddaughter? Since when was that against the law? The necklace was now pulsating heat. It coursed through her body and then into the surrounding air. It met Ida's heat in the air and shimmered imperceptibly.

Rochester took another step toward Mera. As he drew nearer, it felt like a plug had been pulled, sucking the surrounding energy down an invisible drain at her feet. The air became heavy and stale, but the pulsating of the necklace held fast and encircled her body in its invisible current of heat. She breathed deep, like pulling oxygen from a mask. Rochester took another step forward, attempting to move around Ida.

"That's close enough, Rochester," Ida stated in a warning tone.

He stopped, a new comprehension appearing to dawn on him as he studied Mera.

"My daughter said there was something off about her," he said, the smirk returning to his face. "You better be able to control her better than you did her mother, Ida."

Mera's temper met the heavy air, and though she should be quiet, she couldn't help herself.

"I see where Tara gets her charm," she spat.

The smirk fell from Rochester's face, and a shadow passed over his features. The stale air pushed in again. It felt as though she was being covered in concrete, as it thickened and hardened around her. She began to shake.

"Enough," Ida's voice rang out, and under a wave of warmth, the weight lifted from Mera's chest. She drew in a shuddering breath.

"I decide what's enough," Rochester barked, advancing another step toward Ida.

Mera's head was swimming. She fingered the necklace, grateful for its steady pulse tethering her to the ground. Rochester caught sight of what she was holding, and his eyes narrowed.

"My Tara was right," he chuckled, a low, ominous sound. His eyes shone but not with joy. "You think your bloodline deserves a relic like that? After everything?"

Scoffing, he reached his hand out. Mera thought of her

mother, clawing at the air as she screamed in bed at night, trying to bat away invisible hands reaching out to her.

"*Don't touch it,*" she heard herself command.

Rochester's hand dropped. A fog clouded his eyes for a moment. Then he shook his head, his wits coming back to him. He looked up, furious.

"How dare you," Rochester choked out.

Mera's necklace throbbed on her chest while the surrounding air turned solid as stone and encased her entire body. Mera couldn't breathe, and her eyes watered, flooding her vision, but the tears wouldn't fall.

"No!" Ida bellowed.

A surge of heat moved past Mera, and she was suddenly released. She fell to the ground, panting, the tears spilling from her eyes as she struggled to draw breath. She blinked away the tears and saw Rochester on the ground, Ida standing over him.

"You have trespassed here, Rochester," Ida said, terrifying in her rage as she loomed over the sheriff. "You disrespected my family and tried to steal our heirlooms. And now, here, of all places, you attack my granddaughter."

His eyes were almost as wide as his mouth, hanging agape. He extended his arms to keep Ida at bay.

"There are rules—"

"Your invented rules are nothing compared to the ancient laws you have violated. Mera is my blood, and this is our home. Leave and do not come back."

Ida shimmered as she spoke, the warm air stirring and writhing.

Rochester scrambled up, backing away from Ida. "You

keep out of the village, the both of you," he said, making for his car and taking a wide arc around Ida. "And don't ever forget who is in power, or we'll have to remind you."

He climbed into his car, slammed the door, and drove away.

From the ground, panting and shaking, Mera watched his car go. She looked up at Ida with tears streaming down her face, but her back was to Mera as she watched the police car disappear from view. Ida took deep, steadying breaths as her shoulders rose and fell. The air stilled.

"Are you all right?" Ida asked, her eyes flitting to Mera's face then away again.

"I think so," Mera said, her voice cracking.

"I need to close the gate and make a call. If you're okay," Ida said. She hesitated before stalking down the driveway in the gate's direction, leaving Mera to catch her breath on the gravel.

EIGHT

MERA WASN'T SURE how long she stayed on the ground. She wasn't sure of anything anymore.

She put her head on her knees and took deep, ragged breaths. None of what had been happening since she arrived in Convergence was possible. Necklaces couldn't charge your body like a battery. The air couldn't turn to concrete and paralyze you. You couldn't utter a command and bend another person to your will.

A sharp ache stabbed her chest as she realized the one person she wanted to talk to about this was unreachable. Missing. Vanished. Gone.

"Mom, where are you?" Mera sobbed. "What's happening to me?"

A light breeze swept in, brushing gently past Mera. She turned and saw no one, but she realized who was there.

"Ani?"

The air shimmered a few feet away.

"I can't get any closer without Ida sensing me," Ani answered in a voice with an echo, like it was reverberating off a cave wall. "Follow me."

The shimmer was hard to follow as the sun peeked out of the clouds, but Mera heaved herself off the ground. Her body throbbed like a thumb struck by a hammer as she stumbled along the path toward the cliffs.

The shimmer was between the two trees with the stone bench ahead. Mera hesitated, peering over the cliff at the waves, and then followed. The water was clear and calm. She let herself drop onto the bench and looked up in time to see the air beside her quivering, the colors of the wild, cliff-side yard shifting and elongating, taking form. She blinked, and Ani was sitting there.

Ani's eyes were wide, and she stared at Mera, her features pinched in concern. "Are you okay?"

Mera shook her head and closed her eyes. "Well, were you just invisible? My answer depends on that."

"Wow," Ani breathed. "Wow. Grandpa said you'd be clueless, but I thought that Ida would have told you by now. Your mom really never told you, either? Nothing? Wow, that must be so weird, to not know—"

"Ani," Mera said, interrupting her tangent, "not know what?"

"Wow, me?" Ani stood and paced in front of the bench. "You don't even know what you don't—"

"Ani!" Mera cried, jumping up from the bench and standing in front of Ani, who blinked her big eyes at her. "Please, can you tell me what's going on?"

"It's just like, a big responsibility, I wasn't expecting this!" Ani said, shaking her head. "Okay, I have an idea. I mean, if I'm going to tell you, I might as well, right? Just . . . don't freak out, okay?"

Ani extended her hand to Mera. Mera hesitated a moment. She had no idea what was about to happen, but it was the first step to finding the answers to all her questions.

"Come on, we need to go somewhere safe so we can talk. Ida's bound to come looking for you eventually," Ani said, smiling at Mera with her hand outstretched.

Mera took her hand. Ani closed her eyes, and the air whipped to life in a tunnel of wind. The ocean and forest blurred, and Mera became lighter, the distinction between herself and the air around her thinning and overlapping.

And then she swirled away with Ani into the wind.

Mera was now standing in a field with Ani next to her.

Field was the wrong word, she realized as she looked around. They were in a sweeping meadow, a lush rolling green, dotted with flourishes of wildflowers in yellows and reds, blues and oranges. The expanse was met on three sides by a towering forest, dense with tall trees covered in moss with thick canopies of verdant green. On Mera's right, the fourth side opened to the cloudless blue sky. Mera knew the land must give way to the ocean beneath it, as she could hear the far-off waves crashing against the rocks of the cliff.

She gasped. She had been here before. In her dream of the woman with the streak of white hair.

The air was charged. It tingled against Mera's skin. The stirring that had started within her the day she arrived turned into a humming in her bones.

"Don't tell anyone I did that. I could get into a lot of trouble," Ani said. She looked at Mera and grinned. "You can feel it, right?"

"Where are we?"

"The Convergence. It's where the four Elements, well, converge—it's a very literal name. But it's a sacred energy field for Elementals. The village was founded around it," Ani said.

"Elementals?"

"Oh, yeah," Ani blinked at her. "That's what we are. I mean, you are. And I am. We are most sacred and blessed Earthbound beings," Ani said in a formal voice. "We harness the energy of the four Elements. Cool, right?"

"Elementals . . . harness the energy . . ." Mera repeated, but trailed off, more confused than ever.

"Okay, specifics, so—I'm a Sylph, an Air Elemental," Ani beamed. "Salamanders are Fire Elementals, and Terras are Earth. We used to call them Gnomes, but they got all mad about it when they took power, saying no one was taking them seriously. Honestly, that was the least of their problems, at least Gnomes are like, kind of cute—"

"Which one am I?" Mera asked.

"Oh, you're an Undine—a Water Elemental. The second coolest behind Sylphs," Ani smiled.

Wave after wave of incredulity mixed with resignation crashed over Mera with each new detail. She dropped cross-legged on the ground, cushioned by the soft grass. Ani took a seat next to her.

Mera thought of the pulling in her stomach, like ocean waves were moving inside of her. "So, I can like, control . . . water?"

"That would be cool, but no. Only the most powerful Elementals can affect the actual Elements. You're connected to your Element's energy, and each one has its own special qualities. It's what makes every Elemental's powers different. So, Sylphs can use their energy to mimic the air. Hence the invisibility and teleporting."

Mera's mind flashed through everything weird or unexplained that she had experienced before. She thought of objects shaking around her when she was angry.

"I can move things," Mera intoned, then remembered the image of the pulled fire alarm through Ani's eyes. "And . . . did I read your mind?"

"Yes! So cool, by the way. Super powerful Undines can even manipulate the minds of others," Ani chirped. "An Undine's energy is like a current, and your power is to direct it with your mind. Energy conductors, according to my grandpa."

"I'm an Undine. . . . Is my mom one, too? And Ida?" Mera interjected.

"Oh yeah." Ani nodded again. "An Undine is a dominant Element, at least in women If a mother is an Undine, their daughter is an Undine. You all are kind of special that way. You really never knew?"

Mera shook her head. "I guess there were hints that something was strange before, but since I've gotten here, there's all this . . . I mean, I've been feeling—"

"Your powers get stronger the closer you are to your Element," Ani said, gesturing toward the ocean. "And from being in an Elemental community. Most people in Convergence are Elementals. We're the last village in the Northeast, and the most powerful, my grandfather says. The energy here in the Convergence is more pure than anywhere else."

Mera thought of the energy she sensed around some people.

"Wyatt," Mera blurted out when his face swam through her thoughts.

Ani perked up. "Yeah, you know him? He's a Salamander!"

"And the sheriff? Tara and her friends?"

Ani winced. "Terras. They neutralize energy. They're supposed to be a balancing force for all other Elementals, but they've been . . . corrupted, I guess." Ani stumbled over the end of her sentence, trailing off and looking away from Mera.

"What do you mean, corrupted?" Mera asked.

"There was an . . . incident," Ani said. She wasn't looking at Mera as she ran fingers through the blades of grass, which seemed to straighten, electrified, searching for her touch. "No one is supposed to talk about it."

"An incident?" Mera pressed her. "With Ida?"

Ani met Mera's eyes, and Mera could see how scared she was. She thought of the contempt with which the community treated Ida, the anger on Sheriff Rochester's face as he wielded his power against her at the slightest provocation. She needed to know the truth about the Kellen standing in Convergence. It could be a clue to finding her mom now.

But Mera's head was foggy, and it was getting harder to keep her eyes open, the hum of the Convergence louder in her mind now. She swayed a little and closed her eyes to steady herself.

Ani hopped up to her feet. "Definitely time to go!" she chirped, bubbling again. "Your energy must be zapped. You'll need to sleep soon. We shouldn't even be here. Not this close to dark."

She held her hand out to Mera, but Mera had one more question before she would let Ani take her back.

"Do you know anything about my mom?"

Ani crouched down next to her and placed her small hand on Mera's shoulder. "Only what Rochester said. She ran away, and sixteen years later, you showed up."

Mera let Ani stand her up. Taking Ani's hand, the air spun and swirled, and they were pulled into the wind once more.

NINE

ANI AND MERA teleported back to Ida's cliffs, said a weak goodbye, and then Ani vanished into the air. Mera made it up to her room without running into Ida. And Ida didn't come looking for her.

Hours later, Mera was lying on her bed in the gathering dark of the evening, letting the information she had learned wash over her.

At least she had a name for it all now. She was an Elemental. Her family was a part of some incident that corrupted the community. No one knew Mera existed until a few days ago, and it was likely Mera's mother had run away to keep her pregnancy (and Mera's existence) a secret.

She thought for the millionth time of the meeting with Rochester. Mera couldn't stop remembering the wave of heat that went through her as she stood behind Ida during their confrontation. It hadn't been heat—it was energy.

Power.

Another image flashed in Mera's mind—Ida, her long hair flowing all around her body, emanating a glow as her hands moved over an object. For the first time, it all became clear.

She saw what Ida's hands were working over. It was the necklace—suspended in midair, manipulated by the glow extending from Ida's fingers. Ida had turned to look at her then.

Ida must be the reason Mera couldn't remember what came next—why she thought it was a dream. Ani had said that was one of their powers as Undines, manipulating people's minds.

Mera's hands flew to the necklace, still fastened around her neck. She took herself through a list of what had happened since Ida had given it to her. The necklace had brought Mera comfort in the scariest moments. But then why force her to forget? Why not just tell Mera the truth?

Mera took off the necklace, fingers trembling. The moment she unclasped it and pulled it from around her neck, a chill passed through her, like she had just thrown off a blanket. She considered throwing the necklace out of her bedroom window into the water below but decided against it. Mera reached over and laid the necklace on the table by her bed, too overwhelmed to decide.

A sob rose in her throat, and she rolled over to bury her face in her mattress so that the sound wouldn't escape. She could no longer hold in her fear. Fear for her mother. Fear for herself. Fear of being an Elemental—whatever that was.

Mera knew everything would be different now. Even if her mother returned tomorrow, they would never go back to their simple life together. Mera knew the truth about who and what they were, and the loss of her old life hollowed out her insides. She sobbed into her bedspread; the grief wracking her body. She didn't want to be different. She didn't want any of this. She wanted to go home, to be with her mom, but that place didn't exist anymore. Her life with her mom had been a lie, and the memory of it only brought her more pain.

Mera was adrift, seasick, and feverish. She cried until her eyes refused to open. Only then did she fall into a fitful sleep.

***

A pain in her chest made her bolt upright in bed. The full moon was large and bright in her bedroom window, illuminating the room with a pale, ethereal glow.

Her chest seized again and tightened into a knot, doubling her over. The knot clenched tighter and tighter, like a fist had formed where her lungs used to be.

Mera struggled to draw breath in her panic. The short, rasping breaths she was taking pierced her sides. She pushed her hands off her knees and forced herself to stand, her muscles on fire, her entire body rebelling against her.

She needed help.

Mera stumbled toward the door. She broke out in a sweat; the temperature grew oppressively hot as she struggled to exit the room. It was as though the air was trying to hold her back, the heat binding itself to her. But Mera kept moving, propelling herself along the wall—if she stopped now, she'd never muster the strength to start again.

Mera made it out of her bedroom and to the top of the stairs. She took each step one at a time and nearly toppled over halfway down. She took the remaining stairs at a crawl. The air grew denser as she descended, the fist in Mera's chest becoming tighter and growing in size. As she reached the bottom of the stairs, a current picked up in the air. Tiny dust particles floated by Mera on their way to the jet stream, moved through the air by an unseen force.

Mera's eyes followed the dust as it drifted into the cracks in the door of Ida's study. The glow from inside the room spilled out under the crack at the floor. Mera realized with a fluttering in her stomach—Ida, the person she was crawling to for help, was the one doing this.

Mera had a fleeting thought to make for the front door. But then her body seized, and she lost all control over herself. The pain in her body came to a crescendo, spreading from her chest into her head and through her toes. She focused on one thing—making the pain stop.

There was a brief sensation of the energy in her body compressing in her gut like a battery taking a full charge, a momentary respite amid her agony. Then she jerked involuntarily, falling forward and hitting the floor. As her body met the ground, a bomb exploded inside of her. A great wind expanded out of her that sent the entryway's small tables and their adornments, coat racks, and mirrors flying and crashing into the wall, hitting the floor in their fractured pieces.

The fist in Mera's chest released. Mera took her first deep breath in what felt like a lifetime. With that breath, she took in as much life as she could. The air froze, her labored breathing escaping from her in wisps of smoke. She put her hand to her throat as the iciness spread through her body. She convulsed from the cold, her nerves wracked with chills. But as the chill spread, and her heart raced, she felt awake. Alive.

She inhaled again, another ragged half breath. After a few tries, she inhaled deeply. As she filled her lungs with the icy air, the scattered objects moved toward her, surging as though they were being carried on the crest of a wave. They hovered a few feet away before crashing to the ground in front of her. She pulled herself to her feet, surveying the field of debris surrounding her in shock.

The door to the study flew open, and Ida hurried into the hall. She considered Mera with a look of horror.

"What are you doing?" Mera demanded, her voice ragged.

Her heart was still banging away in her chest. The blood pumped in her veins, cutting through the chill in her body like hot knives. The air smelled like it was burning, and smoke was rising from Mera's skin.

"What's necessary," Ida responded in a low voice. Ida put her hand up, and the tightness returned to Mera's chest. "Don't fight it, Mera."

Mera swayed. Her heart was trying to keep beating, but its pace was failing. "Stop it, please," she whispered, a tear spilling out over her cheek, stinging her cracked lips.

"It will be over soon," Ida answered.

The pain burgeoned again, and Mera fell to one knee. Daggers sent chilly jolts into her veins, but this time they joined with the warmth of the blood pumping from her heart. A storm surged in her chest. Mera opened her eyes and looked at her grandmother.

Ida raised her other hand, and the fist squeezed Mera's heart so it felt like it might burst. Mera screamed, lifting her arms to shield herself from Ida. The storm within her unleashed itself through her outstretched hands.

The explosion rocked the house. The windows shattered, the ground quaked beneath them, and thunder cracked and reverberated around the high ceilings of the entryway. All the furniture flew back from Mera, slamming into the nearest wall.

Mera remained still, her arms covering her face, her hands burned and frozen at the same time. When she lowered her hands, she surveyed the damage. Among the wreckage, Mera saw the unmistakable outline of her grandmother's body sprawled motionless on the floor.

Without thinking, Mera sprinted out the door. She ran without purpose or direction, fleeing the house and running deeper and deeper into the dark woods.

TEN

MERA RAN UNTIL she thought her lungs would burst. Flashes of Ida on the ground swam before her no matter how hard she pressed her feet to the uneven earth of the forest. She pushed through intertwined branches and bushes, scraping her arms, legs, and face as she went, but the need to get farther away kept her moving.

Mera reached a small clearing in the woods and fell to her knees, clutching a stitch in her side. She retched, every fiber of her being screaming in pain with the effort.

Through bleary eyes, she looked around the clearing. The full moon was overhead, illuminating the forest, but Mera couldn't make out anything beyond the tree line. She had no idea where she was or how far she had gotten from the house.

Mera's hands shook. She could still feel the rush of power that had exploded out of them. The image of her grandmother's unmoving body on the ground swam to her mind, and she retched again.

Mera was dangerous. An uncontrollable power raged inside her, and she had used it against her grandmother. It didn't matter that Ida had attacked her first, only that it was her grandmother left lying on the ground. Mera had to keep running, though she had nothing with her, nowhere to go, and no one to help her.

Mera was trapped. She longed for her mother.

"Help," she whimpered into the still night air.

There was a glittering on the other side of the clearing. It was slight, but Mera knew she had seen it. A sudden prickling in the air gave her goosebumps. She peered into the tree line and saw it again—a blue orb popping to life like a sparkler.

The light glowed ever brighter as she staggered toward it. She might have been abandoned by her mother and betrayed by her grandmother, but the light would not hurt her. It was humming soft waves of comfort that washed over her as she came closer.

The light wound its way along a path, a beacon in the dark. Mera followed as it steered her around the thorny vines and protruding rocks. The racing thoughts that had been troubling her were gone. Her only thought now was to follow the light. Mera refused to blink, for fear that the light would disappear, and she'd be alone again.

The light flickered further and further ahead of her. Mera had to jog to keep up now, the light zigging and zagging along the rough terrain.

"No, please wait," Mera called, her voice ragged, her eyes stinging against the chilly night air. The light slowed as Mera got closer. "Thank you, thank you," she sighed, relieved.

The light undulated in front of her, its blue glow pulsing and revolving. Mera approached it, smiling. The closer she got to the light, the more she needed to touch it, hold it. She stretched out her hand toward it. When Mera's hand connected with the glow, a shock seized her entire body, as though she had just touched an electric fence. She convulsed and staggered backward, crying out in pain, the spell of the light broken.

Woozy and weak, Mera clutched her throbbing hand. The light hovering in front of her multiplied, becoming two, then four, then sixteen. As the lights split, they surrounded Mera, moving around her in circles. The orbs of light flickered brighter and faster than ever. And then they were upon her.

It was as if someone was holding lit matches to her skin, the orbs pressing and pressing against her face and arms and legs until her insides were on fire. Mera tried to scream, but the lights swarmed into her open mouth, making her gasp and sputter. Mera dropped to her knees, the lights continuing to mob her, glowing now in their malice. She fell forward onto the hard earth, unable to raise her arms to shield herself.

Then, Mera felt a warmth in one of her hands—a firm grip that pumped energy into her skin, pushing the angry lights burrowing into her off in waves. They flickered up and away from her as the warmth spread through her body, until it reached her neck, her cheeks, and flushed her face, expelling the last of the lights. Mera lifted her head from the dirt and gasped deep gulps of the cool night air.

She turned and saw the hand entwined in her own belonged to Wyatt. The warmth from his hand bathed them in a golden glow, the light strongest at the place where their hands connected. The flickering orbs popped angrily, kept away by Wyatt's protection. They hovered for a moment and then floated away into the darkness of the forest.

Wyatt looked at Mera, his eyes warm embers in a

smoldering fire, his hand still clutching hers. "Come on."

Wyatt pulled Mera to her feet. Mera looked at their hands, still entwined, a warm current pulsating where their fingers touched.

"Let's go," Wyatt said, pulling her in the opposite direction of the lights.

Mera took a step and swayed. Wyatt turned and grabbed her shoulders to steady her before she could fall. Through his hands, warmth flowed into her arms, which were scraped and bloody. He took her wrist and placed her arm over his shoulder, then walked them slowly along the path, half carrying Mera. The pain came to Mera in waves as they made their way in silence. Her eyes fluttered, dry and heavy.

"We're almost there," Wyatt said, shaking Mera gently, one hand gripping her waist to steady her, sending warm shockwaves up her side.

"Where are we going?"

"My house, just over here," he said as he helped her over a knee-high stone wall.

They made their way up a small hill, and with a surge of relief, Mera saw a white farmhouse surrounded by a towering backyard garden of flowers, herbs, and vegetables. They walked along a well-worn path from the forest to the garden, lush and glistening in the moonlight. Mera had no idea what time it was, only that it was late. How long ago had she been in the field with Ani? Stepping over Ida's body to flee? Her stomach gave a sick lurch as they passed through the garden and approached the back door of Wyatt's house. What had she done to her grandmother?

"Wyatt," she murmured. She had to tell him what

happened. She didn't want to trick him into giving refuge to a murderer.

"Shh, we should get inside," he whispered, depositing her on the bottom step before moving to open the door.

He came back to help Mera into a small hallway with a staircase on one end and the kitchen on the other. They made their way down the hallway toward the kitchen.

Mera looked at her exposed skin and realized that her bleeding had stopped. Her cuts and burns from the lights in the forest had not healed entirely, but they were no longer an angry red. Mera turned and looked at Wyatt, astonished, and he caught her eye out of the corner of his.

"That's the main Salamander benefit. Tapping into the energy of life," he said with a smile.

A burst of warmth started in Mera's chest and traveled down her arm and into the hand that Wyatt was holding. The warmth kept going, passing from her own hand to Wyatt's. He gasped and pulled his hand from hers, shaking it. Now it was his turn to consider her with a look of astonishment, and then they both stared straight ahead, pointedly avoiding eye contact.

They emerged into the kitchen, with a long wooden island framing a large hearth stove. The house was neat but lived in, the walls adorned with muted paintings of herbs, the shelves with pictures of Wyatt's family, cascading green plants, books, and vases of flowers. Even in the dark, the room emanated that same warmth Mera associated with Wyatt. It felt like a home.

On the other side of the kitchen, Wyatt opened another door that revealed a staircase, leading to what Mera assumed was the basement. Wyatt looked at Mera as though considering how to get her down the stairs. But Mera was stronger now. She felt that familiar stirring of energy in her core. The life was returning to her limbs.

Gripping the railing, they made their way down, Wyatt walking beside her but no longer touching her. She considered pretending she couldn't make it to the bottom without him, so much did she miss the warmth he radiated.

A few moments later, they were in Wyatt's finished basement. There were plush, mismatched couches in a U formation around a large but dated entertainment center. Mera collapsed onto the center couch as Wyatt busied himself in the small kitchenette in the corner, getting them both water. She took in the room, with the same homey touches as the kitchen, and imagined Wyatt here with his family, lounging together.

She thought of her mother and the home they had shared. Here in Wyatt's house, surrounded by the reminders of what she had lost, a fresh stab of grief gripped her, and tears sprang to her eyes.

And that was to say nothing of what happened with her grandmother. A wave of shame came over Mera, and the tears fell in earnest. She didn't belong in this place with Wyatt's family. Mera deserved to be alone. At least that way she wouldn't hurt anyone else.

Wyatt was standing in front of her with a glass of water. She hastily wiped her eyes and took the glass from him.

Wyatt sat on the adjacent couch. "How are you?"

"Better," she said weakly. She showed him her arms where her wounds had begun to heal. "What were those things?" she asked as he looked at one of her burns.

"The reason you never go into the woods alone at night, especially during a full moon," he said, twisting her arm over and rubbing his thumb over one of the burns. Mera yipped in pain and drew her arm away from his touch. "Sorry, sorry," he said, taking her forearm gently back in his hands, "I just need to see the extent of the damage."

He examined her other arm in silence and then said, "Wisps—Will-o'-the-wisps, to be exact. They're all over the woods. They lure Elementals and drain their energy, leaving them for dead. But most Elementals don't fall for it as easily as you did," he added with a smirk.

"Well, to be fair, it was my first experience with demon fireflies."

"What were you doing out there?"

"I was about to ask you the same question. I didn't know any better. What's your excuse?"

"I don't know," Wyatt answered with an earnest shake of his head. "I was sleeping, and I just . . . woke up, and I felt a pull, and I followed it . . ." he trailed off, his warm eyes clouded with confusion. "It's never happened to me before."

He looked pensive for a moment. Mera tried not to notice the way his mouth hung slightly open as he became lost in thought, his lips parted just so.

"I mean, Salamanders can sense the Wisps more strongly, since they're the same energy as us. But I wasn't sensing them at first—that's the weird thing. They were too far away. I must have been sensing—"

His eyes flickered toward Mera and then away again. Mera held her breath.

"—something else, I guess," he finished sheepishly.

"I'm glad you were there," she said. She brought her hand to her face as her cheeks flushed, but she pulled it away again with a painful gasp, her face covered in raw scrapes and burns in various stages of early recovery.

Wyatt leaned close to her to look at the wounds on her face, his brow furrowed. Mera was used to his touch now, but her body still leaned into it, the way a moth finds a light and bumps against it blindly.

"Salamanders just have the right kind of force field to fight the Wisps off, that's all," he said.

"That would explain why you went all glow-y."

"Okay, I'm ready, sit up."

"Ready? For what?"

"Just shut your eyes and hold still," Wyatt instructed her.

"What, why?"

Wyatt sighed and looked at her with annoyance. Mera let out her own sigh and closed her eyes. She kept as still as she could, though she couldn't help but jump as his hands closed over hers.

"Hey," he warned.

"Sorry," she breathed, "it tickles."

He picked up her hands and held them. His energy moved over her skin, a toasty, tingling sensation. It made her blood thick in her veins as it flowed up her arm like lava.

Mera peeked open one of her eyes and saw Wyatt's eyes closed tight in concentration. The golden glow was surrounding them once again. She watched as it came into contact with the wounds on her arm. A slight twinge of pain was followed by immediate relief as new skin covered the wound, leaving her arm healed.

"How are you doing that?" she whispered as he shifted on the couch, coming closer so he could heal the wounds on her face.

"The whole energy-of-life thing," Wyatt explained. "Salamander abilities are more like the sun than actual fire. We accelerate growth. Healing is a natural process, we just speed it up. Or at least, that's what my mom says."

He directed the glow toward the scrapes and bruises on Mera's cheeks and forehead. Mera closed her eyes again and allowed herself to take in the warmth.

When the last cut was healed, Wyatt took his hands from her face, and Mera opened her eyes. Her contented smile fell when she saw that all the color had drained from his complexion. She reached out and grabbed his shoulders to steady him from tipping over.

"Are you okay?" she asked, guiding him as he leaned back on the pillow, his eyes fluttering shut. Panic surged in her chest.

"I'm okay," he said, his voice strained. "Just need to recoup a little."

"You shouldn't have done that, not if it hurts you."

Wyatt opened one eye to look at her. "Either say thank you or just shut up."

"Thank you," Mera said. Then added, "For doing something so dumb."

Wyatt scoffed at her, the color returning in blotches to his face. "Speaking of dumb, why were you in the woods, again?"

Mera laid back into the pillows. She wasn't sure where to

begin, but she needed him to know. She needed it out of her system.

"It's a long story," she cautioned.

"I'm not busy."

With a deep breath, Mera began her story. She started with her mother's disappearance, being shipped across the country to the grandmother she never knew she had, the secrets her mother had kept. She told him about the necklace and her side of the confrontation with his friends.

"I'm sorry," he interjected there. "They're not my friends. One of them is my cousin, and we grew up together, and it's this whole thing with our families—never mind, not important. Keep going."

Mera told him what happened with Sheriff Rochester and her trip to the Convergence with Ani. She got to the part about the incident Ani alluded to that involved Ida and paused.

"She seemed too afraid to tell me," she said, looking at Wyatt expectantly.

"Your family . . ." he paused, and Mera could tell he was trying to find the right words. "There's a very rare, powerful kind of Elemental—Aethers. Every Elemental is bound to their Element, but Aethers . . . they pull from the source of the Elements themselves. Their power is . . . pure essence."

"What does that have to do with my family?"

"Only daughters of Undines can be Aethers."

"Is Ida . . .?"

"No, not Ida. Her sister, Darcy. Something happened. I don't know the details, no one talks about it. But I know that Darcy—she killed a lot of people. Including all the Undines in Convergence. Except for Ida . . . and her daughter."

"*There is no one else*," Ida had told her. The full reality hit her. Mera's family had been murdered by a wildly powerful great aunt.

"How did they stop her? Darcy—if she was all powerful?"

"Ida."

"But if Ida stopped her supervillain sister and lost her entire family . . . *our* entire family . . . then why is she an outcast instead of a hero?"

"I wish I knew more, Mera, I'm sorry. After it all happened, things changed. The Terras took over, and no one questioned it."

Mera's heavy eyelids fluttered. She was more tired than ever.

"You still haven't told me why you were in the woods," Wyatt pressed her after a long silence.

Mera sighed and took a deep breath. She finished her story —her struggle with Ida, her flight into the woods. As it all came out, Mera couldn't believe how easy it was to share her secrets with Wyatt. There was no one who had ever known her like this, other than her mother. Wyatt was a stranger, but he didn't feel like that to her. She realized he never had, really.

"It was you I sensed in the woods," Wyatt said after Mera finished her story.

Mera stared straight ahead for several moments, mustering the courage to look over at him. When she did, he was asleep. Overcome by her own exhaustion, she laid back on the couch and closed her eyes.

ELEVEN

MERA AWOKE TO the sound of a distant phone ringing. She opened her eyes and saw Wyatt still sleeping on the couch next to her. His head was tilted back, his mouth hanging open, and he was snoring softly. Mera lifted her head and looked out the high basement window, shocked to see the gray dawn light filtering through already. Above her, she heard footsteps and hushed voices—the sounds of quiet arguing upstairs in the kitchen.

Mera sat up and seized Wyatt's shoulder, shaking him. He blinked himself awake, looked at Mera with a bemused expression, and then full comprehension dawned on his face.

"Oh no, what time is it?" he asked, scrambling off the couch.

Mera put her finger to her lips, pointing to the ceiling. The voices upstairs went silent. Footsteps tracked toward the basement door.

"What do we do?" Mera hissed as the basement door opened.

"I think we get caught," Wyatt whispered back, watching his parents descend the stairs with a resigned expression.

"Great plan," Mera whispered as his parents reached the bottom of the stairs.

Wyatt's dad crossed his arms and let out an audible huff. Gray dusted his hair, and he was just about the same height as his wife.

"Ooh boy," Wyatt's mom said, looking between Wyatt and Mera. She had the same blackish, wavy hair and warmth as Wyatt. A smile played on her lips even as she fixed her eyes on her son.

"Good morning!" Wyatt said, as if he had just spotted his parents.

They said nothing.

"So, this is Mera," Wyatt said. "Mera, these are my parents."

"Hi," Mera said with a small wave, her cheeks burning.

"Hi, Mera," Wyatt's dad responded, terse but not unfriendly. He was staring at Wyatt, his green eyes narrowing as his son took in the basement furnishings as though they were items in a museum exhibit he had never seen.

"You'll have to excuse Wyatt for a moment. We need a word in the kitchen. Sid?" He gestured for his wife to walk ahead of him up the stairs.

"You boys go ahead, Ned, I'll keep Mera company."

Wyatt stood and followed his father up the stairs. As soon as the kitchen door shut, a steady murmur of admonishment began from the room above. Mera looked at Wyatt's mom, who had thrown herself onto the couch where her son had been sitting and sighed deeply. She looked at Mera and smiled.

"Mrs.—" Mera began, realizing she didn't know Wyatt's

last name.

"Hall," Mrs. Hall said.

"Mrs. Hall, I'm really sorry. Wyatt helped me, and we fell asleep, and—"

"Yes," Mrs. Hall interrupted. "Ida called. You two have a lot to talk about."

Mera sat back, stunned. Ida had called? How would she know to look for her here? But even in her puzzlement, a wave of relief washed over her. If Ida had called, she must be okay.

Through the floorboards, Wyatt's father's voice resounded throughout the house, "*Wisps*? Alone?" and even louder, "You *healed* her? *Alone*?"

Mrs. Hall looked up at the ceiling, a blaze of light flashing in her eyes, making them more orange than brown. "Excuse me," she said, standing and walking across the basement and up the stairs.

"*Completely irresponsible!*" Mr. Hall shouted as the door to the kitchen opened. "*The danger you were both in—*" he continued until Mrs. Hall closed the door behind her.

Mera felt sick with guilt. She had put Wyatt in danger, and now he was taking the full force of his father's anger. Mera crept to the bottom of the stairs, where she could make out the argument happening in the kitchen.

"What is the point of me having these powers," Wyatt was yelling, "if I can't even use them?"

"What's the point?" Mr. Hall bellowed back. "The point is to use them responsibly, only when absolutely necessary, Wyatt, that is the point—"

"She was hurt, Dad! She needed help—"

"No, *you* needed help, Wyatt! You know what could have happened if something had gone wrong. You should have come to us—"

"There wasn't time, you don't understand—"

"No, I don't understand, Wyatt. I don't understand how after your mother and I told you about the kind of trouble getting mixed up a Kellen could bring—"

"Okay, okay," Mrs. Hall's voice cut through their argument. "Wyatt, you need to go get ready for school."

"School? I can't—"

"You can, and you will," said Mrs. Hall. "Go."

"But Mera—"

"We will take care of Mera," Mrs. Hall said, a note of finality in her voice.

Mera heard Wyatt stomp out of the kitchen. The door at the top of the stairs opened too quickly for her to hide, and Mrs. Hall looked at her. She smiled.

"Can you come up here, Mera?"

Mera climbed the stairs, unsure of what awaited her at the top. The Halls had warned Wyatt to stay away from her, and now their worst fears about her had proven true. She stepped into the kitchen and faced Mr. and Mrs. Hall, both looking at her with concern.

"Mera, are you all right?" Mr. Hall asked, exasperated. "A wisp attack is incredibly dangerous. You must be in a lot of pain."

"Oh, I'm fine," Mera said. "Wyatt did a great job, with the healing, and everything." She held out her arms for them to inspect. "See?"

Mrs. Hall approached her, touching her arms in various

places, a small tingle passing through where her fingertips pressed against Mera's skin. She nodded at Mr. Hall.

"Well, good," he said, "but you should know better than to go into the woods at night. The danger you were in . . ."

"I know," Mera said. "I mean, I didn't know before, but Wyatt told me, so I know now. He saved me. I'm sorry I put him in danger, but I didn't know about the woods, I was—"

Mera was about to say she had been running away but stopped herself. She wasn't sure what Ida had told the Halls, but she didn't want to get into the details.

"Ida told us she gave you a big scare last night," Mrs. Hall said, picking up Mera's train of thought. "She was very worried about you."

Mera stared at the floor.

"She wants to explain," Mrs. Hall said, her voice softer.

Mera looked up at Mrs. Hall, tears in her eyes. "Please, I can't go back there. You don't know what she's like."

"Oh, trust me," Mr. Hall scoffed before falling silent again under a withering glare from his wife. A hazy light was breaking on the horizon through the kitchen window.

"Ida isn't perfect," Mrs. Hall said.

"Far from it," her husband muttered.

"But if there's one thing she takes seriously—"

"One thing?" Mr. Hall snorted.

"It's *family*," Mrs. Hall finished. "The most powerful connection we have."

"Ida and I don't see eye to eye, but Sid is right," Mr. Hall said, nodding. "She's not winning any congeniality awards, but you're safest with her, Mera, no matter what has happened."

Mera sighed, but she nodded. She wasn't sold on trusting Ida, but she wasn't ready to discuss that with the Halls, kindness radiating from the both of them.

"Sid, we need to get her back," Mr. Hall exclaimed as a clock in the kitchen struck six o'clock. "We've got to open the diner."

"I'll take her and meet you there," Mrs. Hall replied.

Mr. Hall nodded and walked out of the kitchen. He popped his head back in after a moment, "Bye, Mera. It was good to, uh—well, not good, but—" Mr. Hall paused, lost for words, then shrugged, exasperated, and left again.

Mrs. Hall looked at Mera across the kitchen, her eyes warm and serious. "Mera, it's very important that no one else knows what happened to you and Wyatt last night. Being in the woods at night isn't a rule, it's a law, especially for minors. The Terras—they, well—it's best that no one finds out."

"I won't tell anyone," Mera promised.

Mrs. Hall nodded. "Come on, I'll drive you home."

The word *home* stung in Mera's chest as she followed Mrs. Hall out the kitchen door and to her car.

TWELVE

THE CAR RIDE was quiet, Mera cataloging her anxieties in her mind: confronting Ida, Mr. Hall's assessment of her as dangerous, the trouble she had caused Wyatt.

Every time her thoughts landed on Wyatt, her stomach turned. She stole a glance at Mrs. Hall out of the corner of her eye. Wyatt's dad had made it seem like there was something terrible about her family. Sure, her great aunt had been some super-Elemental, but she was dead, and Ida was a hermit. What danger would that ancient history pose now to Wyatt? She thought of his hands in hers the night before. His sleeping face in the early morning light. Her stomach did another flip.

They found Ida's gate open, still broken from Rochester's visit.

"We heard you had a visitor yesterday," Mrs. Hall said.

As the car pulled within sight of the house, Mera saw that wooden boards covered the first-floor windows.

"Let me walk you in," Mrs. Hall said, unbuckling her seat belt and eyeing the damaged house.

"No, Mrs. Hall, it's okay," Mera said, fumbling for the door handle. She wasn't sure what she would find when she went inside. "Thanks for the ride, and the advice and everything. And I'm sorry again, you know, for what I did— and Wyatt—"

"It's okay, Mera. It's a lot to adjust to," she said, smiling but still taking quick peeks at the house.

Mera knew she had to leave before Mrs. Hall started asking questions. She opened the car door and said, "Okay, well, see you around, I guess!"

Mera shut the door and climbed the steps to the porch. They groaned under her weight. The porch was spotless, missing its characteristic layer of dust. The screen door rested against the side of the house, the metal bent and warped. Mera took another deep breath and walked into the house.

Last night, the scene in the foyer had been one of utter destruction: broken glass and smashed furniture. But like the porch, Mera found the floor spotless, and the framed pictures were hanging again in their rightful places, their glass panes repaired. The furniture was all returned upright, and Mera noticed the lamps had been replaced. The only physical sign of the destruction Mera caused last night were the boards on the windows.

Mera found a letter on the kitchen island in Ida's elegantly slanted handwriting that explained in short, matter-of-fact sentences that Ida was out buying new windowpanes and had called her out of school.

Mera sighed, looking down at herself. Her jeans were ripped, her shirt covered in small, singed holes. Dirt was packed under her fingernails and in the crevices of her fingers and palms. She made her way upstairs toward the shower.

Mera wasn't sure how long she stood under the warm

water, letting the grime from the woods run off her and down the drain. Running her fingers through her hair, she felt where the Wisps had burned it off in pieces, leaving brittle remnants.

When the water turned lukewarm, Mera turned it off and made her way back to her room. She sat in front of the mirror and brushed her hair, the singed edges splaying out as they dried.

Mera looked toward her bedside table and saw the necklace glittering where she had left it last night. She scooped it up, warmth radiating from the chain as she moved it in her hands.

The sound of Ida's car on the gravel drive traveled up to Mera through the silence of the old house. She put the necklace in her pocket and started down the stairs to test this family connection that the Halls had seemed so sure about.

"You're back," Ida said matter-of-factly to Mera, who was standing at the bottom of the stairs when the front door opened.

Mera studied Ida as she entered the house carrying several small bags. Mera looked for any sign of a bruise, a limp or signal of stiffness, but there was nothing. Ida seemed . . . fine. Mera sighed with relief.

"The house looks . . . nice," Mera attempted. "Do you just have a stockpile of lamps somewhere?"

"You think you're the first member of this family to shatter glass in this house?" Ida answered. "Although you may be the first to have shattered all the glass, at once."

Mera flushed red. She thought for the first time of the other Undines who grew up there, learning to use their powers. She thought of her mother.

"Do you like iced tea?" Ida broke into her thoughts.

"What?" Mera asked, surprised.

"Tea. That has been iced," Ida said.

"Oh. Yes."

"Take a seat on the porch. I'll make some iced tea, and we'll talk."

She softened her face into what could not quite be called a smile, but it made her eyes as kind as Mera had ever seen them. Mera half smiled back and made her way onto the porch while Ida walked back toward the kitchen with her shopping bags.

Mera settled herself into one of the plush cushions of the wicker lounge chairs, facing the intersection of the cloudless blue sky over the ocean. A breeze picked up off the water. August was almost September, and the tips of the leaves were tinged red and yellow. They swayed on the branches, fluttering in the wind. Mera hugged herself in the porch's shade.

"You need a coat," Ida said, emerging on the porch with two glasses of iced tea.

"I've never needed one," Mera replied with a shrug. "Mostly."

Mera thought of the winter they had spent in Colorado when Mera was eight, and her mom's pledge never to see snow again. After that, they had stayed in the southwest on the outskirts of one desert or another.

"Genevieve always hated the cold," Ida said.

Mera looked over at her grandmother, who was staring off toward the water. Maybe she wasn't the only one missing her mother, after all.

"So, you know now? What you are?" Ida asked.

"An Elemental. An Undine," Mera sighed. She glanced at Ida, who pursed her lips together.

"I'm sorry about last night," Ida said, turning to face Mera. "It was not my intention to hurt you."

"What was your intention?"

"I was binding you. To prevent you from using your powers."

Mera sat back in the chair. She thought of the way her body seized up around the fist in her chest the night before. She remembered how she had fought against it. The struggle with Ida, the explosion that blew out the windows.

"My powers," Mera repeated.

"I did not send myself flying through the parlor door."

"Sorry," Mera muttered. "But—"

"I could feel the power radiating from you when you got out of the car the first day," she said and then paused. "To be truthful, your strength surprised me. And . . . it frightened me."

"I scared you?"

"Our powers can be dangerous, and you have already been using them—"

"Not on purpose! I didn't even know!"

"Which is why I had to bind you! It's a long-practiced ritual, meant to block an Undine's access to their abilities."

"I felt like I was dying. I couldn't breathe. Couldn't you have sat me down and had a conversation with me before going with magical suffocation?"

"It's not magic," Ida huffed. "And you shouldn't have been able to feel it, let alone fight it. But, evidently, you did."

Evidently. Mera's anger burned again, but she saw Ida's hand shake as she raised it to take a long sip of her iced tea.

"Well, I could have come to you, too, I guess," Mera said finally.

"Trust does indeed run both ways."

They sat together in silence for a few moments.

"What were you doing in your study the other night?" Mera asked. "With the necklace?"

Ida looked at her. "You remember that?"

Mera shrugged, and Ida let out a great sigh.

"The necklace I gave you was your mother's, that part is true, but it's also an object of great significance in the world of Elementals. We call them Wards. The one you have is very rare. You saw how Rochester reacted when he saw it."

"And his daughter, too, at school. She tried to take it."

Ida bristled but composed herself again. "It's an ancient, treasured object, and it has been in the care of the Undines for centuries. And that night, I was reawakening its energy."

"Oh, naturally," Mera said, as if Ida had just told her she had been cleaning it.

"It's a powerful protective token, and I just had this hunch that you might need it," Ida said, the smallest suggestion of a smile playing at the corner of her mouth. "I thought if you remembered seeing me using my powers, it would frighten you, and you would be too afraid to wear the necklace."

"Yeah, that sounds about right. That's why I took the necklace off."

"That explains how the Wisps were able to get to you. . . ." Her eyes flitted upward. "And your hair, it seems. Where is the necklace now?"

"In my pocket."

"Good. It's better to be wearing it, but always keep it with you. You'll need it."

The early afternoon sun had shifted to its high noon position, bathing the lawn and trees behind it in a glittering light.

"How did you find out?" Ida asked.

The necklace warmed in Mera's pocket, and she knew now was the time for total honesty. She took a deep breath before telling her grandmother everything that happened with the day before: her trip to the Convergence with Ani, and then her conversation with Wyatt last night. Ida listened, pursing her lips at the risks Mera had taken, but did not interrupt. When Mera got to the part where Wyatt had told her about Darcy, her story stuttered to a halt. She searched Ida's face for a hint of a reaction, but her grandmother remained stoic.

"You are trying to get into my mind. Do you realize you are doing that?"

"What?" Mera sputtered. "No! I was just reading your expression—"

"It is one of the most challenging Undine powers to develop. The mind, of course, is incredibly complex and difficult to navigate. But you are a natural, I'm afraid."

"I'm sorry—I didn't—I just thought I was good at reading people. . . ." Mera trailed off.

Ida nodded again. "To tap into someone else's mind, to influence their will—my mother used to describe it as navigating a ship in the middle of a hurricane. It takes incredible fortitude. It does not come naturally to me, and I have always been very fortunate for that. It came too easily to

Darcy."

Mera shivered again, but this time it had nothing to do with the breeze. "What happened to Darcy?"

"Darcy was given an incredible gift, and it consumed her."

Ida turned to face Mera as she said this, and their eyes locked. An image flashed through Mera's mind—a wild-looking woman, her eyes ablaze, standing in a hazy scene among rubble and destruction, a guttural scream tearing from the woman's throat and reverberating in Mera's mind. Mera shut her eyes, and the woman was gone. She wasn't sure if Ida knew what Mera had just seen—if it was something Ida had given to her, or that Mera had taken.

"And then the Terras took control," Ida continued. "They're supposed to be incorruptible, a balancing force in the community. But after Darcy, everyone was afraid. And a young, ambitious Adam Rochester was right there to capitalize on their vulnerability. The honorable Sheriff Rochester, he crowned himself."

"And they punished you for what happened with Darcy."

"Banished me. Rochester said Darcy's rampage proved that they were the only ones to be trusted with any kind of power. A council of representatives from each Element always ran the village. As self-appointed sheriff, he reformed the council, naming only Terras to govern. He passed strict, new laws and named his supporters to other positions of power. His supporters make up most of the police force."

"But why would he want to be sheriff?"

"We are Elementals. We derive our powers from the laws of nature. These sacred laws formed our communities, gave us our gifts. They are the pillars of our village. And so, to be sheriff, Rochester believes that he is the law. He can arrest us, put us in jail, force us out of the village. Keep us from our people, separate us from the greatest source of our abilities. Take them away."

Another scene flashed in Mera's mind—the wild woman from before, but not undone. She was youthful, tall, her light blond hair floating as if suspended underwater. Beside her stood another woman with curly auburn hair. They were holding hands, towering and emanating a sheen of power that warped the air around their bodies, enveloping them in their might.

Mera blinked, and the image of her grandmother and Darcy vanished. Ida stared out across the lawn, over the cliffs. Ida, who had taken on an Aether and won, who destroyed her own sister for the good of the community. The people of Convergence should have looked at her as their savior, but Rochester took Ida's sacrifice, her betrayal of blood, and had used it to crush her.

And now here she was, their broken warrior, the village witch in her haunted house. Someone to fear. Waves of heat rose from Mera's body as the anger bubbled inside her, until it permeated the surrounding air, stretching out like elongated fingers.

"Mera," Ida gasped, "you must learn to control your powers. Rochester will look for any reason to punish you. He is the most dangerous kind of man—a man with as much fear as he has power. Promise me you will be careful. That you will learn to control your power."

"I promise," Mera said, and she meant it. She relaxed, and the heat subsided within her.

Ida stared at her for a few more moments and then nodded. They settled back into another stretch of silence, but something was tugging at the corner of Mera's mind. Ida said Darcy was gifted at reading minds and emotions, and that she let her powers control her. She asked Mera to promise she wouldn't do the same thing. Mera's stomach clenched, her heart beating faster.

"Ida, when did you know Darcy was an Aether?"

"From the moment she was born."

Mera shuddered and looked up at the sky, clear only moments before, now covered in swirling dark clouds. Mera saw Ida's expression darken as she, too, turned and looked up.

"We should go inside," Ida said, standing.

Mera jumped as a bolt of lightning flashed in the clouds above her. She heard Ani's voice in the back of her mind. *Only the most powerful Elementals can affect the actual Elements.* She forced herself to stand, her anxiety stiffening her muscles.

As she walked into the house, fear knotting up her stomach, her mind swirling with unpleasant suspicion, it began to pour.

***

The rain fell as Mera and Ida settled into the dining room for lunch. Mera took her seat, grateful for the grilled cheese and tomato soup in front of her. She had been wishing for this meal since her mother had vanished. It was what her mother would always make during a storm. Mera could hear her voice in her head—

"Rainy day food," Ida said, cutting into Mera's thoughts.

Mera looked up, stomach fluttering, and her grandmother smiled at her before returning to her own grilled cheese.

They ate, and Mera admired the room once again, following the intricate carvings around the walls, her eyes landing on the elaborate fountain in the center. Suddenly, she understood.

"It's the Elements," she said.

Ida looked up at her, her spoon halfway to her mouth.

"The walls," Mera said, her voice rising with excitement at her discovery. "They represent the Elements."

"Well, yes."

Mera paused for a moment to let her irritation with her grandmother's general personality subside then turned her attention to the floor-to-ceiling windowpanes with the etchings of the hourglass and people flying through the air. *Sylphs*, Mera thought. Her journey with Ani seemed so long ago, even though it was just yesterday. She could see the similarities to her friend in the engraving on the glass, the slight figures leaning into the air.

Friend? Mera thought. Is that the right word? She had only just met Ani, and—

"Can Sylphs *fly*?" Mera exclaimed.

Ida stared back at her, her bland expression answer enough.

Mera rolled her eyes. "Oh right, invisibility and teleportation are on the table, but flying would be absurd."

"Not every Elemental in the same Element has the same power, and no one can fly," Ida said. "Some are born with no abilities. It all depends on their connections—to the Element, to themselves, to their family, and to the community. That's what matters."

Mera's eyes flitted to the wall behind Ida, with the ocean and its sea glass figurines passing water between them, a shimmering chain of cooperation and fluidity.

"Are we really the only Undines left?"

"In this village, yes."

"Where are the other villages?"

"All over the world. But I've never been. I've never left this one."

Mera put down her spoon. "You've never left this village?"

Ida shook her head.

"Not even on vacation?"

"No, never."

"Not even—"

"Never, Mera," Ida responded, the edge back in her voice.

"But . . . why?" Mera sputtered before she could stop herself. She couldn't imagine someone like Ida being stuck in one tiny village her entire life, never mind this one.

"Elementals are not like other people. We must live in secret. The danger an Elemental faces in the outside world— the Wisps you encountered were only the beginning."

Mera considered what she said, spooning more soup into her mouth. "There are other creatures, like the Wisps?"

"Yes, but they're not the only threat. We stay in the village because our community keeps us safe—"

"This community?" Mera scoffed. "They've imprisoned you in your home!"

"Oh, there are much worse things than being banished. We are protected here by our shared Elemental bond. The village was settled on a very powerful space of Convergence—"

"Where all the Elements meet, I know," Mera interrupted.

"Yes, well, when we're here, at our strongest, our energy forms a kind of border. A force-field that keeps out the things that wish us harm. The stronger our community bond, the stronger the protection. Even in these fractured times, the village is the safest place for us."

Ida stood to clear their plates. Mera sat back in her chair and gazed out the window, listening to the sounds of the rain. She felt as though she had aged a decade since she arrived just a few days ago.

"I suppose it's time we get started," Ida said from behind Mera.

Mera turned and found her grandmother had returned to the room, carrying a handsome wooden box. The wood was glossy, but the rust on the hinges belied how old the box must be. Ida set the box in the middle of the table and opened it. She extracted a feather, a marble, and a circular weight. She placed the three objects in front of Mera, taking extra care to keep the marble steady. Ida moved the box off the table, setting it to the side.

"Up, please," Ida instructed.

Mera stood, and Ida whisked her chair away then returned to Mera's side.

"From my observations, you have the most trouble with gauging the intensity of your power."

"Meaning?" Mera asked, irritated that Ida was already leaving her behind.

"Meaning you broke everything on the first floor last night."

"Oh, right, that intensity."

"For our first lesson, I want you to use your powers to

move these objects—one at a time. Each requires a different technique, and a different amount of force to move. Allow me to demonstrate."

Ida held up her hands, as though she were about to play an invisible piano. Ida fixed her gaze on the feather, and she made a slow, soft beckoning gesture with two of her fingers. The feather lifted off the table and swept into the air, following the movements of Ida's fingers. Ida guided the feather back onto the table.

Next, Ida moved onto the marble, using the same technique with her hands. The marble rolled around, making figure eights and other designs as Ida dictated with small flicks and swirls of her fingers.

Ida moved to the weight, which she picked up and maneuvered through the air just as easily as the feather. She placed the weight back on the table and turned to face Mera, who clapped. Ida rolled her eyes.

"It is important to channel your energy through your hands. That is essential to being able to control your power, and the object. Focus your mind on how you want the object to move, and then use your hands to conduct them, just as you would if you wanted to physically pick up one of these items."

Mera nodded as though she understood any of what Ida was saying. She turned to the objects on the table. She was afraid to call on her powers to do anything. Ida was right— she had no idea how to control them.

"Mera," Ida's voice cut into Mera's worries, "you must let go of everything else that you are feeling when you use your powers. Your energy must flow uninhibited by any fear or anxiety. It is already there. Find it moving within you—find it at your core."

Mera closed her eyes and concentrated. She knew what Ida meant—that sensation she had been having ever since she arrived in Convergence. Of something stirring and waking within her. She focused on the ebbing and flowing of energy that started behind her navel and prodded it ever-so-gently with her mind. It responded and grew, moving through her chest and into her shoulders, then down her arms, and into her fingertips. Sweat broke out on her forehead, dripping down her back, the effort of keeping the energy inside her hands causing her body's temperature to increase in waves.

"Breathe, Mera," Ida said, her voice sounding far away.

Mera took a shaky breath then exhaled. The pressure in her fingers relaxed a little. She took an even deeper breath in and out. The energy pulled away from her fingertips with each inhale and then returned with the exhale. It reminded Mera of the tide, going to and from shore. Mera understood—if she were to flex her palm and extend her fingers, the energy would release. She breathed in and out, in and out.

"Now focus on the feather," Ida instructed.

Mera opened her eyes and looked at the feather on the table. Cautiously, she extended her hand out in front of her, her muscles shaking with the effort of her control. It surprised her to find that her arm was heavier than usual, as though the energy it now housed had its own mass.

Mera focused on the feather, extending her fingers out toward it. In her mind, she willed the feather to rise. She moved her fingers in the same beckoning motion that Ida had used, but nothing happened. The feather remained on the table, unmoved.

"You'll have to release some energy, Mera," Ida said. "Your hands are the conductors. The feather will not move unless your energy connects with it. Just enough to lift it—a gentle touch will do."

Mera nodded and turned her attention back to the feather, sweat now running down her face. Her heart was pumping blood and energy around her body at such a speed that Mera started to panic. How was she supposed to control the strength coursing through her? It was brimming in her fingertips like water in an overflowing dam, and she was not sure she could stem the tide of power wanting to escape.

"Mera," Ida commanded in a stern, clear voice, "you have the power to stop what you're doing now. Do not lose control."

"I'm trying," Mera hissed through gritted teeth. An image flooded her mind of her great-aunt, feral with power.

"Your powers are you, but you are not your powers. You are in control. Focus!" Ida was now yelling over the blood rushing in Mera's ears.

Mera closed her eyes again, tears falling from the corners in her exertion. She forced herself to breathe and pressed her arms to her sides, focusing on pushing the pulsating, radiating heat from her fingers back into her core. A coolness spread through her, driving the heat away. The chill spread, pushing the energy back to the pit of her stomach until it was just a small pull.

Mera exhaled, relief flooding through her. She swayed on the spot and leaned against the table to steady herself. She opened her eyes and looked at her grandmother, who was equally relieved.

"Well, that could have been worse," Ida said.

Mera shook her head as her grandmother collected the objects from the table. Ida closed the latch on the wooden box just as Mera's legs began shaking.

"We'll try again after school tomorrow. You should rest," Ida said, holding the wooden box now.

Mera nodded. Although it was still early afternoon, she felt like she could fall asleep on the dining room table.

"You did well," Ida said and then swept from the room.

Mera dragged herself up the stairs. She hadn't moved any of the objects, but for the first time, she understood what it meant to control her powers. And what was more, she could do it again.

THIRTEEN

TWO HOURS BEFORE sunrise, Mera was already awake. In the last twenty-four hours, she had slept more than she had been awake. Her body was stiff and sore, but she was rested for the first time since she had arrived at Ida's.

She tiptoed toward the kitchen, not wanting to wake her grandmother, but stopped short at the bottom of the stairs. The boarded-up windows had been replaced with gleaming glass panes. And through the one closest to the front door, Mera could see Ida standing on the porch, staining a large china cabinet. It was still dark, but Ida had two work lights hung up to see by.

"Do you sleep?" Mera asked, stepping outside onto the porch.

Ida didn't startle or even turn. "I've found that the older I get, the less sleep I need."

"Is this for the house?"

"No, I repair items for the antique shop in town. For a fee, of course."

"I was wondering what you did all day."

Ida turned and gave her a withering stare. "Yes, restoring

furniture is what I do all day. Others call it a job. I was also left a large sum after the passing of our family."

"Oh, sorry."

Mera watched as Ida continued to work. She would rather live paycheck to paycheck for the rest of her life than to rely on an inheritance at the expense of losing her family. She knew Ida felt the same way.

"I've been thinking about what you said yesterday, about the community being the safest place for Elementals. Mom and I lived on our own for so long. . . . Is that what happened to her? One of those . . . creature things got to her?" Mera asked in a rush. It was this that had woken her and refused to let her rest again.

"Urban areas, or somewhere like the desert, would have served as a good shield for an Undine. It would have prevented her, and you, from accessing our Element, from allowing anyone else to sense your powers. Even me."

Ida pursed her lips, then continued. "When Genevieve left here, she did so in the middle of the night. I didn't understand why until months later, when I received a letter with no return address. All it contained was a picture of you."

"So she left because she was pregnant with me," Mera said, keeping her voice as level as she could. "But why?"

"If Rochester had known, if he had suspected the birth of another Undine, another Kellen . . . I imagine she ran away to protect you."

Mera shut her eyes and let out a deep sigh. That sounded like her mother. And it also sounded like she hadn't been fleeing Ida, after all.

"And my father?" Mera asked, a hint of defiance in her

tone.

"I have no idea, Mera."

Mera hadn't been expecting an answer. Her mother had always outright refused to discuss the topic, and investigating her paternity wasn't high on her list of priorities at the moment.

"Mom ran away to protect me as a baby—do you think that's what she's doing now? Running away? To protect me?"

"That I don't know, but—I believe she's alive," she finished.

Mera decided that Ida wasn't the type to indulge herself in frivolous hope. If Ida believed her mother was alive, too, then that was enough evidence for Mera.

Mera sat, watching her grandmother's careful brush strokes as the sun rose in earnest. After some time, Ida glanced up at the brightening morning light.

"You'd better get ready for school," Ida said. Mera left Ida to finish her cabinet, her mind still lost in the small hope her grandmother had given her.

***

It felt like ages since Mera had been to school, even though she had only missed one day. Ida had dropped her off without incident, reminding her about their lesson after school. Mera was early enough to get around to her classes before the first bell to collect her missing assignments.

When the bell rang, Mera was already in her seat in calculus, working on the previous day's homework. She knew she would run into Tara and her cronies at some point, who were sure to be fired up about Mera's meeting with the sheriff. Mera was hoping to put it off for as long as possible.

And though she would love to catch a glimpse of Wyatt or Ani, the only friendly faces in town, she knew she would have to avoid them, too, if she was destined for a life of social isolation, like her grandmother. Mera supposed now was as good a time as any to get really good at math.

She was focusing on a line graph when she sensed someone standing over her. Mera looked up, and Ani was there.

"Mera!" Ani chirped, throwing herself into the seat next to her.

"Hi Ani," Mera said. She would have to be direct—Ani didn't seem like the type who would take a hint.

"I'm so glad you're here—is everything okay? When you weren't here yesterday, I almost went to your house, but I was afraid Ida would be there, and—"

"Ani," Mera interrupted her. "We have to talk."

Students started trickling in from the hallway, Ms. Powell hurrying them along.

"Yes, we definitely do. There are so many other things to tell you. I'll find you later today!" Ani smiled and sat back in her seat just as Ms. Powell started handing out a quiz Mera had forgotten about.

The rest of the morning passed in a fog. Aside from learning that she came from a long line of ancestors with a supernatural connection to the sea, Mera could not stop wondering about her mother and what her disappearance meant. Her thoughts kept finding their way back to Rochester —an enemy of her family, the reason she would have to tell Ani and Wyatt to stay away, and possibly the reason her mom had left Convergence in the dead of night in the first place.

Last but not least, Darcy plagued her thoughts. There was still so much she didn't understand about her great-aunt.

In the cafeteria, she sat at a table in the corner by herself, reviewing the notes she had taken in calculus earlier in the week to gauge how badly she had bombed that quiz. She looked up, puzzling through a calculation, and saw Ms. Hughes walking across the cafeteria toward her. Mera reached for the necklace in her pocket, and with a pang of anxiety, she realized she had forgotten it in the pants she had worn the day before.

"Mera!" Ms. Hughes called to her while still several tables away, waving as she approached. Students turned and snickered.

Ms. Hughes sat on the bench across the table from Mera, letting out a big sigh and smiling. "I'm so happy to see you're feeling better. I heard you were out sick yesterday."

Mera nodded and tried to turn her grimace into something that could pass for an expression of greeting.

"I was worried—I hope things are okay at home," Ms. Hughes said.

"Oh yeah," Mera said, affecting a casual air. "Some kind of stomach bug. Lots of puking. Very gross. I don't think I'm contagious, but . . ."

"I'll take my chances," Ms. Hughes said with a conspiratorial wink. She leaned in closer. "What I wanted to talk about, Mera, is our friendship. It disappointed me when Principal Crowley said we wouldn't be meeting anymore, and I hope that there isn't someone trying to prevent us from . . . connecting."

Mera blinked at her, remembering Ida's pledge to put an

end to her sessions with Ms. Hughes. The silence stretched between them, Ms. Hughes staring, her smile straining.

"Well, anyway, I just wanted to let you know that my door is always open to you, if you need someone to talk to."

Mera nodded and muttered a quiet thanks, returning to her notebook. She could sense that Ms. Hughes hadn't left. She looked back up at her.

"In the meantime," Ms. Hughes said, her voice low and less cheery, "I'll be sure to . . . check up on you from time to time. Make sure everything is going smoothly for you at school—and home."

Ms. Hughes gave her one last big smile and then walked away.

"What was that about?" Wyatt asked, dropping down into the seat Ms. Hughes had just vacated.

Wyatt's eyes were searching her face, alight with concern. Mera leaned toward him but stopped herself.

"Are you okay? When you didn't show up yesterday, I wondered—"

"I'm fine," she said with what she intended as a casual shrug, but she gestured too emphatically with her right arm and knocked over her open water, dousing her math notes and the table between them.

She cursed and jumped up from her seat as water cascaded off the side of the table and into her lap. Wyatt leapt up as well, throwing napkins from his lunchbox onto the puddle. Mera grabbed her notebooks and was shaking the water from them when she heard a table erupt in laughter. She looked to her left and saw the Terra table howling at her misfortune. Tara and her friends were yelling something to Wyatt that

Mera couldn't make out, but she could tell from Wyatt's expression that he could. The warmth he was exuding moments before had turned into a dangerous crackling. A lump formed in Mera's throat.

"Thanks for . . . everything and all, but we shouldn't—we can't—I can't be friends with you," she said, grabbing the rest of her things and shaking as much water from them as she could. "I'm sorry, I have to go."

Wyatt looked up at her in surprise, his angry expression replaced by one of hurt. He looked from her to the Terras and opened his mouth, but Mera hurried out the side door before he said a word.

Mera sped away from the cafeteria and didn't stop until she was in the deserted trophy hallway. She slumped onto the floor, taking deep breaths to quiet the storm building inside of her. Mera wanted to stand her ground, but something happening to Wyatt or Ani, or to Ida, was too great a risk. Her mother had run away to keep her safe—she wouldn't betray her sacrifice by taking chances to flirt with a cute boy. Even a cute boy who sent non-Elemental-related butterflies to flutter in her stomach every time he looked at her.

Mera sighed and took stock of her math notebook. She gathered her damp materials and made her way to the library to recopy her most recent notes to a new notebook. She found a secluded table in the vacant periodical section and got to work.

Ani dropped herself into the seat across from Mera and pulled out her schoolbooks. Mera looked up, and Ani flashed her a big smile before opening her chemistry book.

"Um, Ani?" Mera said in a low voice.

"Hmm?" Ani responded, already absorbed in her chemistry assignment.

"I appreciate you explaining everything to me the other day, and I know you could get in a lot of trouble for doing that, so thank you, but—"

"That was so cool, wasn't it?" Ani interrupted, still working.

"Yes, super cool," Mera said. "But I know how dangerous it is for you to be seen with me, I know how the community feels about my family—"

Ani scoffed.

Mera grew impatient. This wasn't easy, but she needed Ani to understand. "Ani, seriously. With Rochester, and Tara—it's not safe."

Ani looked up at Mera. She put down her pen. "The Terras have never accepted me. I used to try so hard to be their friend, but it just . . ." Ani stared at her hands, without words for the first time. She continued with a sigh. "They look down on Sylphs, always have. They think I'm just some airhead."

"But your family—"

"My family, afraid of Rochester?" Ani exclaimed. "Plus, hello, I'm already on their bad side because of the whole thing with the fire alarm."

"I don't want anything to happen to you. Being friends with me isn't worth the trouble."

"Mera . . . my whole life here, I've always been on the outside of things. Without anyone ever noticing. Like I'm . . ."

"Invisible," Mera finished. Ani looked up at her, her big eyes brimming.

"When you showed up, it was the first time I felt like that could change. And *that* is worth something to me. Like, worth a lot to me actually." Ani smiled softly. "Plus, with how messed up this place is, I'm looking forward to a little trouble."

Mera laughed despite herself. She shook her head. "But . . . are you *sure*?"

"Mera, please," Ani whispered. She threw Mera one last exasperated look before returning to her textbook. "This is a library."

Mera saw the corners of Ani's mouth twitch. She watched Ani work for a few moments, and then she smiled, too. A weight lifted from her heart. She worked in quiet comfort across from her new friend, the Sylph.

FOURTEEN

LATER THAT EVENING, Ida and Mera were sitting next to each other on the porch—the feather, the marble, and the weight on the wooden table before them. Mera's mood had improved since their lesson yesterday, having spent the rest of the afternoon at school in the company of Ani, who made the ever present Terras easier to laugh off. She also refastened the necklace as soon as she had returned home. It hummed against her chest.

"You're happy," Ida said, a note of accusation in her voice.

Mera shrugged. Her grandmother looked at her suspiciously for another moment and then stood.

"Let's walk," she said, sweeping down the front steps toward the path to the cliffs.

"I thought I'm not allowed near the cliffs!" Mera called after her, hurrying to keep up on the trail.

"You are not!" Ida yelled over her shoulder. "But today we will make an exception."

They continued walking until they reached the cliff overlooking the ocean then settled onto the bench.

"It has been a very long time since an Undine needed

training," Ida said. "I realize I may have skipped an important step in helping you master your powers.

"The most ancient teachings tell us that as an Undine, our nature is most like the sea—at times, peaceful and harmonious, and at others, turbulent and destructive. It is our choice which qualities we choose to harness and manifest."

They both looked out over the cliffs. From here, the sea seemed perfectly placid, stretching endlessly to the horizon, the water moving in rhythmic waves in front of the setting sun.

"It all comes down to self-control," Ida said. "Self-control is a choice you will have to make over and over again. You must bend the energy to your will and prevent it from taking you over. There are times when it will take all the strength you have."

The energy within her stirred, as though awakening to Ida's challenge.

"I don't say any of this to scare you, but to prepare you. You've experienced your power in its wildest form—after it has taken you over. It is a different thing entirely to be the one in control. You must discipline yourself to work as one with your energy. Only then will you be at peace."

Mera looked out onto the sea, but now she heard the waves slamming into the rocks below them. The image of the black spot in the waves she saw days ago flooded her mind— bleeding larger and larger, churning into a frenzy. Mera's breath became harder to draw in, like she was being dragged under the surface. The necklace burned on her chest.

"Self-control," Ida urged.

Mera exhaled and refocused on the ebb and flow of the tide

in the distance. The rhythm of the waves moved within her, having been there all along. The tug of going out to sea, the pull back into shore. The energy, moving in time to her heartbeat, was a second pulse.

The ocean—spread out before her, moving within her—was always stirring, never settled, not even for a moment. It was a feeling Mera had experienced her entire life but had never put into words. She looked at Ida with tears brimming in her eyes.

"I'm ready to try again."

Standing in front of the objects on the porch moments later, Mera sensed the energy of the sea within her, but this time, it felt like hers.

Mera held out her hand and willed the energy up from her core and down through her arm, pushing and pulling it like the tide. Mera extended her fingers, focusing on the feather and sending her energy out of her body. It found the feather, moved underneath it, and pushed it off the table. The feather floated upward until it was suspended in front of Mera. With a flourish, she moved the feather to her extended hand and took it out of the air. Her energy flowed back into her, nestling itself into her core.

Mera looked at Ida, eyes wide. Ida only nodded. "Now the others."

The marble moved easily. She rolled it over the table, first back and forth, and then in figure eights until Ida cleared her throat, and Mera made the marble go still again.

The weight proved trickier than the other objects. It was heavier than Mera had imagined, and after maneuvering her energy underneath it, she couldn't seem to lift it. Mera knew she could release a torrent if she wanted to, send the weight flying from the porch all the way to the cliffs. Instead, she closed her eyes and found her heartbeat, taking deep breaths. Her energy matched the slower pulse of her heart. She knew it was safe to pull more of it from her core and press it toward the weight. The weight rattled on the table, but Mera met its resistance with clean waves of increasing intensity, escalating in force, until the weight lifted from the table as the feather had.

Mera smiled, swirling the object around in the air, the energy purring and building inside her as she conquered the weight. She guided the weight back to the table and let out a long breath. She flung herself back into the porch chair, exhausted.

Ida smiled and started gathering the items back into the box. "We'll pick up again tomorrow. Dinner on the porch?"

Mera watched the late evening sky turn from a smoky blue-gray to sapphire, taking in the distant sounds of the water and the animals in the forest readying themselves for night. As the yard darkened, small lights flashed through the trees in the distance. She wondered if they were fireflies or something more sinister, but her necklace was emitting a steady warmth, and she knew she was safe there.

Ida reemerged with two plates, which Mera accepted gladly. The exertion of their lesson had left her ravenous.

"I see you're wearing your necklace again," Ida observed as Mera shoved another forkful into her mouth.

"I forgot to put it on this morning. Didn't even realize it until Ms. Hughes cornered me."

Ida paused her eating but didn't look up. "And what did

Ms. Hughes have to say?"

"That we wouldn't be meeting anymore, but that I could always see her if I needed someone to talk to."

"I told you I would see to that."

"She's not an Elemental, right? She's just, like, a person?"

"No, she is not an Elemental."

"Okay, so do you have an issue with all guidance counselors, or is there something about Ms. Hughes—"

"Do you trust me, Mera?" Ida interrupted.

"I want to," Mera replied honestly.

"Then please trust I have told you everything you need to know about Ms. Hughes in telling you I do not trust her."

Mera considered her for a long moment. "Fine. But you have to tell me some time."

"Only if it's necessary, and let's hope it never will be."

FIFTEEN

AND SO PASSED the next few weeks for Mera—school all day, and lessons with her grandmother at night.

"Wow," Ani gasped when Mera explained their progress. "You're being taught by *the* Ida Kellen. I can't even imagine what that would be like. My grandfather just wants to read to me out of these books, won't let me try anything. Has anyone ever read a book about metaphysics out loud to you before? It's torture."

Mera laughed. "What would you do, if you could try anything?"

Ani's eyes glittered. "As if I could pick just one thing! There are so many of these like, amazing Sylph rituals. There's one to summon a spirit, one to travel between dimensions, one to look into the past—"

"Woah, what?" Mera asked, stunned.

"I know, right? I told you Sylphs are awesome," Ani bragged with a shrug.

School was tolerable now that she had Ani as a companion. The Terras still glowered at them from doorways and neighboring tables, but they seemed less inclined to bother them when Ani and Mera were together. The unspoken agreement among the Elemental students to ignore Mera's existence was still in full effect. A few weeks after their conversation in the library, Mera remarked on it to Ani as they sat down for lunch.

"Most of them ignored me long before you got here," Ani said with an eye roll. "Or they'd call me like, phantom-girl or airhead or some other very clever insult."

"But *why*?"

"Sylphs are difficult for other Elementals to understand, especially our earthbound overlords. The Terras see us as weird eccentrics, out of touch with reality. And everyone else just follows suit."

"I'm sorry they treat you that way. It's not fair." Mera placed her hand on Ani's arm. "Aren't there other Sylphs in Convergence?" Mera looked around the cafeteria, half expecting to see one or two flying around.

"Not many anymore, other than my family and Wyatt's dad's side, and a few others," Ani said, shrugging. "Most moved out when the Terras came to power, high-tailed it to an Elemental community in South Carolina. I've been a few times, but Mera, the bugs down there are like, mutants. One time I saw this moth, and I swear it blinked at me—"

Ani could sustain herself on a topic like mutant bugs for several minutes without assistance, so Mera allowed herself to wonder how Wyatt was doing. Though she had tried to push him from her mind, she often found her thoughts floating back to him.

Since the incident in the cafeteria, they had barely even looked at one another, though Mera was constantly looking *for* him. She found him sitting alone a few times at lunch but forced herself to hurry away, stared down by Tara and her cronies as she went. It was the least Mera could do to spare Wyatt and his kind parents the consequences that would come from being associated with her.

But nothing took up as much time and energy as her lessons with Ida, which were becoming monotonous. Each day, three new objects appeared for Mera to test her powers on. She moved the objects with little effort now, and she felt ready for the next step, whatever that was. But Ida had other ideas—she was adamant that Mera continue learning to control her powers on a smaller scale.

"And when will I be deemed in control?" Mera asked that afternoon, impatient after another hour of turning paperweights over in the air.

"When you can control your powers without thinking," Ida said, standing on the other side of the table, as if watching Mera move small to mid-sized desk ornaments with her mind was a treasured pastime.

Despite her annoyance at her grandmother's slow release of responsibility, Mera was anxious at the creeping distance growing between them. Aside from her bland but unwavering attention during their lessons, Ida seemed preoccupied. She hadn't taken on any new restoration projects, and Mera often found her staring out one of the first-floor windows, brow furrowed as though she were straining to see something in the distance. Seeing Mera watching her in the reflection, Ida would mutter something about "meditating" and sweep from the room.

Mera suspected that her grandmother wasn't sleeping. The

week before, a rhythmic banging awoke Mera, and she burst onto the porch just in time to see her grandmother emerging from the walkway, toolbox in hand, explaining that she'd made repairs on the gate by moonlight.

On other nights, Mera heard Ida moving around each floor of the house at all hours. Every evening, her grandmother's feet padded down the hardwood third-floor hallway. She would pause at Mera's door and then move on. Mera imagined her pacing in slow circles around the perimeter of the house and would find her each morning, asleep in a chair, facing out the window. Her grandmother was waiting for some danger, and though Mera suspected it was Rochester, Ida had remained silent about her stressors.

Mera herself was struggling at night, vivid nightmares keeping her awake. When she used her powers, she was opening a deeper part of her mind, but she hadn't yet figured out how to put it back to sleep, not even on the night before her biology exam. As soon as she closed her eyes, the dreams played on an endless, vivid loop, unlike any she'd ever had before.

She was standing in the middle of the Convergence. It was dark, the air humid and charged, little sparks tickling her fingertips. She stood between two figures, both cloaked in fog and shadow. She sensed a power emanating from the two of them, electrifying the air.

Mera looked to the figure to her right. Warm waves radiated from the figure. It tickled at first, creeping up her arm like goosebumps, but then a splash of heat caught her around the wrist and burned. She took a step away, closer to the figure on her left. The air from this side swirled like a vortex. Cold air moved toward the figure as though it were being pulled, then pushed back away, filling Mera with a deep chill.

The figures stepped forward, and their bodies twisted. The air between them exploded, their streams of hot and cold connecting and erupting in a dazzling display of light. Her body boiled and froze, melted and shattered all at once.

Every night, Mera bolted up in bed, sweating and shivering. The dream never changed, but no matter how many times she saw it, she couldn't make sense of it.

She thought it'd be better to keep the dreams to herself, but Ani proved difficult to keep anything from. She had taken to staring at Mera while they were supposed to be working on their homework in the library during lunch, their now regular reprieve from the cafeteria. The Terras weren't big readers, it turned out.

"What's wrong?" Ani asked Mera one afternoon after a long bout of staring that Mera had tried to ignore.

"Nothing," she muttered and kept working.

"Ah-hem," Ani coughed.

Mera looked up at her again. Ani was sitting with her arms crossed, giving her a look that Mera knew meant she wouldn't let it go.

"Well," Mera sighed, "how much time do you have?"

Once Mera started talking, she found it hard to stop. The dreams, Ida's tense behavior and weird sleeping patterns, the vague threat of Rochester and the Terras hanging over her, on top of everything she was going through with her mother's disappearance. Much like when she had confided in Wyatt, it all came pouring out.

"Oh," Mera said, carried away now, "and did I mention I moved to a village full of nature-magicians?"

Ani rolled her eyes but leaned in close. "Mera, that sounds really serious—"

"Uh, yeah, you think?" Mera said. Seeing the concern on her friend's face, she felt a pang of guilt for saddling Ani with all of it. "I mean, yeah, I know."

"Grandpa Vihaan has been saying he can sense something coming," Ani said in a low voice.

"Your grandpa can see the future?"

"Not even *nature-magicians* can see the future. But my grandpa is a super powerful Sylph. He's sensitive to what goes on in the village, the shifting energies and all that. He's been picking up on something lately."

"What do you mean?"

"I'm not sure—I mean, he's not sure—but he says it's in the air, and it's like, not good."

"So you think it's all connected then? My dreams, Ida, whatever your grandfather is sensing?"

Ani just stared at her.

"What?"

"Nothing," Ani said, looking down at her hands.

Mera counted backward from five in her head. By the time she got to three, Ani looked like she was about to explode.

"What if you aren't dreaming? Didn't you say you can't tell when you're going all mind reader? What if you're seeing what's in Ida's mind? I mean, Elementals accidentally use their power in their sleep all the time. My grandmother's sister teleported herself into this locked storage room in their barn, and no one could find her for days—"

"Ani," Mera interjected.

"They had to come up with this special blanket for her to use. It was supposed to ground her energy while she slept, but then a few weeks later they found her sleeping in the gazebo in the town square—no one even knows how she got out from under the blanket, it was like, really heavy—"

"ANI."

"Oh," Ani said, as if she had just realized Mera was there. "Sorry."

"You think I'm picking up on Ida's thoughts?" Mera asked.

"Or her memories. Which would mean that you might have a front-row seat," Ani said, leaning in closer and dropping to a whisper, "to the greatest Elemental showdown in history."

"She can sense stuff like that, me in her head. She would have put a stop to it."

"Unless she was really tired and preoccupied! And if she trusts you now, she probably wouldn't be guarding against it."

The way Ani described it made Mera feel like a thief. Like she had stolen into her grandmother's most private thoughts. And if it was true—if what Mera was seeing in her dream was Ida's tragic battle with her sister—that must mean . . .

"Ida is thinking about this every night?"

That meant her grandmother was torturing herself relentlessly with this memory.

The two sat there for a few minutes in silence. Mera held the charm of her necklace in her fingers. It radiated soft waves of heat deep into her chest. She closed her eyes and tried to savor the small comfort. When she opened them, Ani was staring at her.

"What is it?"

"No one has ever known what happened between Ida and Darcy. Ida's never spoken about it."

"I've been having the same dream for weeks, and I get no further than the moment it begins."

"Well," Ani said, almost bouncing in her seat with excitement, "what if there was a way to stay in the memory? All the way to the end? I mean, come on, the biggest moment in Elemental history, and no one knows what happened, but we could! I mean, you could! But then you could tell me." Ani's eyes were alight with the possibilities she saw before her. Then she faltered. "You'd tell me, right?"

"I can't," Mera said, shaking her head and standing. The guilt made her limbs heavy as she started jamming her textbooks into her open bag.

"But this is important, Mera! This could change everything! And you could do it, we could practice!" Ani continued. She jumped out of her seat and grabbed Mera's last textbook, forcing Mera to look at her. "Maybe we could help her!"

"I can't, Ani!" Mera snapped, the force of her voice surprising even her. She snatched her book from a stunned Ani and turned on her heel to leave.

"Mera, wait! I'm sorry!" Ani called, but Mera was already gone.

SIXTEEN

MERA AVOIDED ANI for the rest of the day, though she had a feeling her friend was keeping her distance. Mera needed space. And she needed to speak to Ida.

But Ida's car wasn't waiting for her in its usual spot after school. Mera's skin prickled as she walked up and down the patch of sidewalk where Ida always waited for her.

Mera wasn't sure what to do, so she sat on the bottom stair of the school's now deserted front steps. She was calculating how many miles it would be to walk home when the front door of the school opened accompanied by a burst of voices. Mera turned to see Wyatt in front, his head bowed, hurrying down the front steps. Behind him came Tara and her friends, calling after him.

"Hall!" one of the Terras yelled. "Come on, dude!"

Wyatt spotted Mera, stopping short. She stood and faced the Terras. Her necklace hummed.

"Oh, perfect," Tara said. "This is who you're rushing off to see?"

Mera glanced at Wyatt, who was now staring angrily at Tara.

"Choose your side wisely, Hall," one of the boys called.

"There are no sides!" he called back.

"No sides?" Tara yelled. "I'm sorry, whose family went on a murder spree and took out half the population, again?"

"That has nothing to do with her!"

"It has everything to do with her!" Tara screamed.

The surrounding air thickened, the reverberations of Tara's anger all around them. Wyatt's usual friendly glow was coming off him in a dangerous flicker. Guilt flooded Mera's stomach.

"Don't," she pleaded to Wyatt.

But Wyatt's eyes locked on Tara.

"Okay, I can take a hint!" Mera yelled up to the Terras, her voice muffled in the thick, tense air. "I'll go!"

She held up her hands as if in surrender and turned to leave. As soon as her back turned, Tara's hatred radiated through her thoughts like a sonic bomb, and the air turned painfully still.

An electric charge cut through the stillness. She turned to find Wyatt had moved in front of her, his hand outstretched toward Tara and her cronies. They raised their hands toward Wyatt and Mera, the stale air deadening even more around them. A flickering emanated from Wyatt's hand like a solar flare, keeping the inert air at bay. A static charge filled the space between them.

Wyatt looked at Mera—his eyes shining yellow. He extended out his other hand to her. Just as she reached to take it, a new voice filled the air.

"*What is going on here?*" Mr. Hall jogged toward the front steps of the school, his car door ajar.

Wyatt's hand dropped, and the air returned to normal. The Terras exchanged nervous glances. All except for Tara, who stared daggers at Mera.

"Mr. Hall, we were just—" one of the Terras attempted, but Mr. Hall put his hand up.

"I saw what you were doing, Clay, and your mother is going to hear about it, as well. As for the rest of you—" Mr. Hall fixed his stare on Tara for a moment, and she stared back defiantly. He turned to Wyatt and Mera.

"You two, in the car. Now."

Wyatt and Mera hurried to the car. Mera cast one last look at Tara, whose face was contorted in anger. As she slipped into the back seat and buckled up, relief and gratitude welled up inside her before the anxiety set in. Mr. Hall and Wyatt made a clear choice by rescuing Mera, and she couldn't help but worry about the consequences for them.

"Thank you," she said, her breathing still shaky.

"What were you two thinking?" Mr. Hall exclaimed. "And are you all right?"

"We're fine, but see, Dad?" Wyatt cried.

"Yes, Wyatt, I saw it, but—"

"*I know*, Clay is my cousin—"

"Your only cousin!"

"My only cousin. And family is important, and eternal bonds, and blah blah blah. But there are more important things than family."

"Do not let your mother hear you say that."

"I don't care what you and Mom think anymore. I'm done bowing down to the Terras," Wyatt said, the heat in the car rising.

"Ah," Mr. Hall said, "so you're physically fine, just delusional."

"This isn't funny, Dad," Wyatt exclaimed, heat flaring again.

"You're right, Wyatt, it's not funny. What you're saying is dangerous. We are already walking a fine line with the Terras, and now, you and Mera just had a showdown at high noon with the sheriff's daughter. So excuse me as I try to process."

"I'm sorry," Mera said from the back seat.

Wyatt whipped around, annoyance flaring in his eyes. "What are you sorry about?"

"For the showdown at high noon!" Mera exclaimed. "For getting you involved!"

"You didn't get me involved in anything. You've been ignoring me for weeks, remember?" Wyatt huffed, turning back around in his seat.

It had been three weeks and two days, in fact. She caught Mr. Hall's eye in the rearview mirror and her face flushed.

"I just didn't want you to have to deal with—well, that," she mumbled.

"Oh, thanks. Foolproof plan," Wyatt replied sarcastically.

The energy coming off Wyatt was radiating something more than annoyance. Mera stretched her senses and found a deep layer of loneliness buried beneath his anger. Mera was the reason he had separated himself from the Terras, and then she had left him alone.

"I thought I was protecting you. But I realize now that I only hurt you."

Wyatt turned to face her.

"I'm sorry," she said again.

He stared at her for another moment, and then his eyes softened, and he sighed.

"Fine," he said, turning and facing forward again as the temperature in the car cooled ever so slightly.

Mr. Hall was again looking at her in the rearview mirror. There was concern for his son and family, wading into open conflict with Rochester and the other Terras. Concern for Mera, this young girl, losing her mother and then being dropped into the Convergence minefield that had both nothing and everything to do with her. It wasn't her fault, just like it hadn't been Ida's all those years ago. But this slow-simmering war had started with their bloodline.

Mera shook her head. She realized she wasn't reading his expression—she was reading his mind. She forced herself to look out the window, away from the rearview mirror.

"I'm sorry, too, Wyatt," Mr. Hall said. "You're right. There are more important things. And I'm glad you stood up for something more important today."

A few more moments of silence passed, and Mera watched the tree line thicken as they moved further out of town.

"That was a nice shield," Mr. Hall said to Wyatt.

"Is that what that was?" Mera asked. "That flickery thing?"

Wyatt turned around and fixed her with an incredulous stare, and Mr. Hall snorted.

"Yes, that flickery thing was a shield," Mr. Hall said. "They're protective energy barriers, but not every Elemental can do one. Sylphs, my people, can't do them. Terras can't either. But Sals here—"

"Dad," Wyatt interjected. "Please stop calling us that."

"Salamanders then," Mr. Hall said, rolling his eyes.

"They're pretty good at them. Undines, too."

"But I still don't get it, Dad. Why are the Terras doing this? I've never seen anyone act like this, never mind all of them."

"I have," Mr. Hall muttered.

"Rochester?" Mera asked.

Mr. Hall nodded. "Narrow in on a target, close ranks, shame the non-believers. It's kind of his thing."

Mera didn't have to read his mind to know that he was thinking of her grandmother once again. The guilt on his face told her all she needed to know.

They arrived at Ida's driveway, the newly installed lock in place on the closed gate. Mera gathered her backpack and extracted the key that Ida had made for her the week before. Mera thought it was a good sign the gate was closed.

"You can just let me out here," she said, reaching for the door handle. "Thanks for the ride, Mr. Hall."

"Of course!" he exclaimed, spinning in his seat to face her. "Listen, maybe we can have you and Ida up to the house for dinner sometime soon."

Mera thought she sensed a tinge of embarrassment, like the invitation was long overdue. Wyatt gaped at his father.

"Oh, well, I'll have to ask Ida, but I'd like that. Thanks!" Mera said. She looked at Wyatt. "Talk to you at school tomorrow?"

"Talk to you at school tomorrow," he said and flashed her a small smile.

Mera blushed and jumped out of the car, nearly toppling into a pile of leaves on the edge of the driveway in her haste to exit. She gave a meek wave to Wyatt and Mr. Hall as she unlocked the gate and walked through it then locked it behind her. She made her way to the house as they backed the car out onto the road.

As she approached the house, anxiety replaced the momentary lightness from her reunion with Wyatt. Her grandmother was the one who had insisted Mera meet her right after school. What had kept her from picking Mera up?

Mera entered the house and listened, but it was silent.

"Ida?" she called, but there was no response.

Mera walked down the hall, peered into the drawing room, and let out a sigh of relief. There was Ida, asleep in a plush armchair by the window. Mera's relief at finding her grandmother safe was replaced with annoyance. She was glad that nothing terrible had befallen Ida but irritated that her grandmother's insistence that "nothing is wrong" was now leading to her nodding off in the middle of the day. If there was an impending threat, how was Ida planning to defend them if she was napping?

Shaking her head, Mera put down her backpack and moved toward Ida.

"Ida?" she whispered. "Ida, wake up."

Mera placed her hand on Ida's shoulder to shake her awake, but as soon as she made contact with Ida, an image seized control of her mind. The house disappeared, replaced by the darkness of the Convergence. This time, Mera wasn't between the two figures but off to the side. One figure stood over the other, and with a flash of lightning, Mera saw the upright figure was Ida. Darcy had her hands raised, her face streaked with blood and tears. She looked into her sister's eyes as Ida bore down on her.

"Please," Darcy begged. "Ida—"

"The time for mercy has passed, Darcy."

"Think of Genevieve!" Darcy screeched as the energy emanating from Ida's hands doubled in intensity. "What will happen to her?"

Ida pulled back her hands, and for a brief second, Mera thought her grandmother was going to relent. But then she said, "That is the only thing I'm thinking about," and summoning one last surge of power, she struck at Darcy's heart. Darcy let out a terrible, heartbreaking wail.

Mera's hand jerked from Ida's shoulder, and she stumbled backward, bumping into the side table behind her and knocking over a lamp. The sound shocked Ida awake. She jumped up, throwing her hands in a waving motion, unleashing a furious blast of power in Mera's direction. Mera's necklace sprung to life and gave off its own burst of energy to match Ida's. The forces collided in midair and sent Mera sailing backward into the wall. She slumped on the floor, her necklace radiating heat, searing her skin.

SEVENTEEN

MERA'S EYES FLEW open. Ida leaned over her, stroking her hair.

"Oh, thank goodness!" Ida cried.

Mera scurried backward on the carpet, trying to find her footing. Ida leaned away from her, startled.

"Mera, it's okay!" Ida said. "It's me!"

The two stared at each other for a moment.

"Are you okay?" Ida asked, concern on her face.

Mera assessed herself. Despite the bruise she was sure would form from where her back hit the wall, she was physically fine. But she had also just watched her grandmother murder her great-aunt while she begged for her life.

"No," she said, an edge to her voice. "I'm not."

Ida nodded, her eyes lingering on the hole in Mera's shirt from where the necklace had burned its way through. "I am very sorry, Mera, it was not intentional—"

"Which part?" Mera snapped. "You falling asleep and forgetting to pick me up from school? Or blasting me halfway across the drawing room? What happened to always being in control of your powers?"

Ida paused. "It will not happen again."

"That's it? No explanation?"

"There is no further explanation. I apologized and assured you it will not happen again."

"Tell me what's going on. You aren't sleeping. You patrol the house all night and stare out the window like you're waiting for some attack."

"That is none of your concern," Ida responded, meeting the hysteria creeping into Mera's voice with a flatness in her own.

"Yes, it is!"

"You are acting like a child," Ida said, making for the door.

"I saw your dream!" Mera yelled, desperate.

Ida froze. Mera feared Ida might blast her again, but she was more afraid of Ida icing her out. Ida's last words to Darcy had been about Mera's mother. What if her mother's disappearance had something to do with this moment, with Darcy? Ida was the only one with the information she needed. The only one who could explain why, with Darcy defeated, she had struck a fatal blow, and what that decision meant for her mother's safety.

"I didn't mean to," Mera continued to Ida's back, "but I did. What happened? With Darcy, that day at the Convergence—what did I see, Ida?"

"Keep out of my mind," she said and swept from the room.

***

The ride to school the following day was silent, tension filling the air between them. Ida parked across the street from the school, as always. Before getting out of the car, Mera's eyes swept the entrance, looking out for the Terras, but the coast was clear. Mera turned to Ida, as though she had remembered something.

"Oh, I forgot to mention. I joined Homework Club."

Ida looked at her, disbelief etched into the features of her face.

"Homework Club," Ida repeated.

"Yeah, my friend Ani runs it," Mera said.

That much was true. Ani was the founding and only member of the Billings High School Homework Club and had been begging Mera to join. Homework Club met in the library after school, because that's where Ani did her homework every day.

"It meets until four thirty."

The top of her skull tingled. Mera realized that Ida was trying to see for herself if Mera was telling the truth. Mera pushed the thoughts of homework to the front of her mind, along with the memory of Ani pleading with her to join the club. Ida blinked and looked away, satisfied.

"Four thirty," she said.

"Great," Mera said, hopping out of the car.

As Mera made her way into school, she considered how guilty she should feel for deceiving her grandmother. Such a complex duplicity coming naturally to her was not something she wanted to celebrate, considering what Ida had said about Darcy.

She found Ani standing by her locker.

"Mera," Ani said as she approached. "I'm sorry about yesterday—"

"No," Mera said, cutting her off. "You were right."

Mera looked around to ensure that no Terras were close by

and took a step closer to Ani. "I have to tell you something."

"Oh," Ani chirped, bouncing on the balls of her feet, overcome with conspiratorial excitement.

"Ida is hiding something. There's more to what happened with Darcy that day. And . . . it has to do with my mom."

"Oh wow," Ani whispered, her eyes glittering. "But I told you, no one knows—"

"I have an idea."

Ani gasped. "Reading her memories?"

"Well—"

Ani gasped again. "Reading her *thoughts*?"

"No—"

Ani gasped again, and Mera covered her mouth with her hand.

"No!" Mera exclaimed. "I saw into her memory yesterday —Ani, shh, listen she'll never let her guard down around me again. I can't count on getting back into her mind. We'll have to see for ourselves."

Ani's eyebrows furrowed in confusion.

"We need to go back in time."

***

Ani gaped at Mera like a fish every time they locked eyes the rest of the morning.

"Didn't you say Sylphs can look back into the past?" Mera asked Ani, leaning across their lab table amid the bustle of the teacher collecting their homework in Chemistry. Ani stared at her for a moment before her gaze floated away again.

Ani maintained the same far-off look throughout their morning classes until Mera was ready to give up on her plan. If it sent Ani spiraling this far into the clouds, it might be too out there.

When the lunch bell rang and their math class filtered out into the hallway, Mera and Ani walked side by side. They allowed the other students to hurry past them then turned to each other simultaneously.

"Forget I said anything—"

"Here are all the reasons this plan is absolutely bonkers," Ani cut Mera off. "First, you can't go back in time, that would be ridiculous. You look back in time by doing a ritual, and only very powerful Sylphs have been able to do it.

"Second, the ritual would require participation from every Element, and like, do you know any Terras lining up to help us? They would turn us in for even bringing it up!"

"Okay, but—"

"*Third*," Ani pressed on, "what happened between Ida and Darcy at the Convergence is an incredibly powerful event— Sylphs way stronger than me already tried to see it! The energy that was unleashed that day is like, impenetrable."

By this time, the two had made their way through the hallways and into the library, taking a seat at their usual table.

"Fourth, and most importantly," Ani continued. "So much can go wrong. You can go blind or catatonic, your brain left in the past. Can you imagine, Mera? Your brain. In the past."

"If you don't physically go back in time, wouldn't it be your mind, not your brain, that gets left in the past?" Mera questioned.

Ani threw up her hands. "Even worse!"

"How is that worse?" Mera argued.

Just then, Wyatt slid into the seat next to Mera.

"Um, am I interrupting something?" he asked, looking

between the two of them.

Ani was wearing an expression of almost comical discomfort.

"I'm torturing Ani with my ideas for Homework Club," Mera said.

"Dangerous, borderline suicidal ideas," Ani hissed at Mera.

"Like what?" Wyatt asked, pulling out his lunch.

"Time travel," Mera said, matter-of-factly.

Wyatt laughed. "Well, I guess I picked the right table."

Ani looked from Mera to Wyatt, her eyes the size of silver dollars.

"Ani, Wyatt won't turn us in to the Terras."

"Says who?" Wyatt asked.

Ani turned white as a sheet.

"Sorry, sorry!" Wyatt exclaimed, seeing Ani's expression. "Ani, I promise, I won't say anything to the Terras about your Homework Club being a front for Mera's time travel agenda."

Mera and Ani both looked at him. His laugh faded.

"Wait, you're serious?"

Mera nodded, and Ani shook her head.

"Mera," Ani cried, exasperated, "did you not listen to anything I said? About your brain slash mind?"

"I heard you. You said it's impossible."

"Yes, I did!" Ani said, banging her fist on the table for emphasis.

"But you also told me you've always wanted to try it. So you must have considered some workarounds before, right?" Mera coaxed.

"Well, I mean, a few like, theories."

"I know that it would be dangerous. But I need to know what happened between Ida and Darcy that day at the Convergence," Mera said. Wyatt tensed up next to her, understanding the severity of what he had stumbled upon. "Something happened that has to do with my mom's disappearance, I'm sure of it."

"I might have a workaround for some issues, but I don't know how we'll ever get all the Elements represented. We would need all four."

"You have a Salamander," Wyatt said. Mera looked at him, surprised. He gave her a solemn smile. "If it might help find your mom, then I'm in."

"You'll need to join Homework Club," Mera said, smiling back at him.

"Done."

They looked at Ani, and she nodded.

The weight of what they agreed to settled on the table. Then Ani gasped.

"What is it?" Mera asked, looking all around. She could feel Wyatt's body temperature jump up several degrees, his arm so close to hers on the library table.

"Now that we have three members, they'll put Homework Club in the yearbook!"

EIGHTEEN

THE DAYS TURNED into weeks as Mera, Ani, and Wyatt worked to figure out how to do what only a few Elementals had done before—look into the past.

It took Ani a few days to get used to Wyatt's presence in their small group. Mera casually remarked on this to Ani one day as they walked to meet Wyatt in the library.

"I mean, you kind of can't help but like him, right?"

"Maybe *you* can't," Ani giggled.

"What does that mean?" Mera felt herself go red. Ani just kept giggling as they approached Wyatt sitting at their usual table. He looked up at them.

"What's so funny?" he asked with a grin. Ani only laughed harder until she was shushed by the librarian.

They decided it would be too risky to meet in the library or anywhere in the school. The danger of being overheard was too high, and the consequences were too severe. Since Mera and Wyatt's showdown with the teen Terras, Tara and her gang had been keeping their distance. Mera worried they were plotting something.

Instead, Ani brought them to a grove of trees on the

outskirts of the woods, beyond the school grounds. From their vantage point, they heard the whistles and yelling from the football field nearby but were hidden from view by the dark trees at the forest entrance. Mera shuddered, remembering the last time she journeyed into the woods.

Mera, Ani, and Wyatt settled in the grass, and Ani dumped the contents of her backpack into the center of their triangle. Instead of her usual textbooks, her backpack was filled with aged but pristine notebooks.

"These are the diaries of the wisest Elemental in a thousand years, Mana Joshi. Not bragging, but she was my great-grandmother," Ani said.

"Did she look into the past?" Mera asked, picking up the one closest to her and flipping open the cover. Inside, the book was covered in elegant scribbles and hand-drawn diagrams.

"Or into the future?" Wyatt said, reaching for a notebook.

"Well, no, she didn't have any powers, technically. They never developed."

Mera and Wyatt exchanged a glance.

"But she dedicated her entire life to documenting the history of Elementals. She's like, a very famous Elemental scholar."

"Oh yeah, I remember seeing these before!" Wyatt said. "On that Vanguard field trip to your grandfather's library in fourth grade."

"Vanguard?" Mera asked, holding in a laugh.

"It's a club for Elemental boys. Preparing them to be future leaders," Ani explained with an eye roll.

"You do different levels of training, and you get awards for it," Wyatt interjected with a shrug. "Anyway, these were all in that cabinet in the library."

"Oh?" Ani said, averting her eyes and organizing the stacks.

"Behind glass."

"Hmm," was all Ani said without looking up.

"Locked glass."

"Ani," Mera studied her friend. "Did you . . . steal these?"

Ani looked up, a mischievous smile breaking across her face.

"Ani!" Mera gasped, equal parts shocked and impressed.

"Let's just say, I might have found a creative way around a lock or three," Ani said, trying to affect an air of nonchalance. "But like, we're not going to do anything bad with them. It's a scholarly pursuit. I'm sure Grandma Mana would be pumped we are using her work to do something so massively cool. They've just been sitting there."

"Wow, Joshi," Wyatt said. "I'm not sure the Vanguard would approve of that."

"It's a good thing the Vanguard is non-inclusive, and I am free to ignore their patriarchal code of honor," Ani chirped. Then, to Mera, "I tried for years to petition them to allow girls in the group."

"Did the petition work?"

"They were all blah blah tradition blah blah," Ani sighed. "Elementals love their nonsensical, problematic conventions."

"Who doesn't?" Wyatt added.

***

As they worked through the diaries, their conversations about the ritual often transitioned into them telling stories of their own. Ani had plenty of tales about her little brother, like when he learned how to turn only his head invisible to scare their mother. But he got stuck that way for a whole week until her grandfather figured out how to reverse it.

Wyatt talked about his odd-couple parents—a Sylph and a Salamander—and their absurd disagreements in the course of running the town's lone diner. Their most memorable was when his father accidentally killed his mother's tomato plants by spraying them with an "organic growth aid" of his own invention. When his mother found out, she banned him from the garden but has caught him on several occasions sneaking back in to test out new variations of his spray.

Mera recounted stories of life with her mom, like the time a bird got into their apartment. Her mom shrieked every time the bird came near her and suggested they simply move instead of trying to get it out.

As the three of them laughed together, a tickle warmed Mera's core. Something new was growing there, taking root in an empty place inside of her. She had only ever felt this close with her mother. And now her mother was gone. This thought snapped Mera back to reality, and she found herself always being the one to refocus them on the task at hand.

It took weeks to sort the pertinent information in the diaries from the irrelevant. Ani's great-grandmother's handwriting was easy enough to read, all neat loops and crisp lines, but the structure of the diaries was difficult to decipher. They were a collection of cerebral ramblings, textbook-like recitation of facts, fragments of thoughts, and complex diagrams that sometimes turned out to be doodles. Ani's scattered manner of communication was an inherited trait, as was her brilliance.

From what the three had gathered, Ani's great-grandmother believed that looking into the past was possible, but it involved one of the most ancient Elemental rituals in known existence.

"Hang on," Mera said, flipping a journal over to read the cramped notes in the margin of a busy page. "This says we don't need a Terra to do the ritual!"

She handed the journal off to Ani, who bent over it. "Oh my god, you're right! '*A Sylph can harness the wind to the past, if guided by the other three Elements, in person or symbol.*' We just need a Terra object!"

Ani pulled out her yellow legal pad and flipped to a new page with a flourish. "Adding '*powerful Terra object*' to our To Be Determined list."

In another journal, Wyatt came across a passage that explained the ritual would have to happen in a place where all four Elements combined, supercharging their powers. There was even a large illustration of such a location on the adjacent page that Mera recognized—the Convergence.

"There's no way," Wyatt exclaimed, slamming the diary closed.

"Why not?"

"It's too out in the open," Ani said. "People go there all the time."

"We would get caught," Wyatt affirmed.

Mera closed her eyes and let out a long breath. "Another item for the To Be Determined list, I guess."

The next issue was more beguiling. Mana wrote that Elementals could only look into the past through a great disturbance of the ritual place.

"Okay, adding to the list and moving on!" Ani chirped. "This next part is about '*anchors*.' It says we'll need an anchor to the present, to ground us in our current time and place. Do you think it means, like, physically anchor, or metaphorically? Oh, wait, it says it will also have to connect us to the moment in the past we're trying to access. So, metaphorical. But like, also physical."

Wyatt frowned, flipping through one of their dozens of notepads.

"Something that grounds us in the present and connects us to the past . . ." he repeated.

"Okay, so what counts as an anchor?" Mera asked.

"Doesn't say," Wyatt sighed.

"Well, let's keep moving forward," replied Ani, her voice cheery as she scratched onto her notepad.

"How can we keep moving forward? Everything's a dead end," Mera snapped.

Her skin tingled with a warm, sharp energy that Mera recognized as her irritation. The air pulsed with her annoyance. Her face flushed red, and she closed her eyes, taking a few deep breaths. She hadn't had a flare up like this in weeks, thanks to her training with Ida.

"Sorry, I didn't mean to . . ." she muttered at Wyatt and Ani as she opened her eyes and saw them staring at her, looks of surprise on their faces. "Ani's right. We need to keep going."

The air returned to normal as she steadied herself.

These unsolvable riddles were stressful enough, but Mera had plenty of other things going on that put her on edge.

At home, things were as tense as ever. It took a monumental effort for Mera to keep the pretense of normalcy with her telepathic grandmother. Her mental guard was constantly up to make sure that Ida never glimpsed her work with Ani and Wyatt. Every moment of protecting her secret from Ida took a level of mental and emotional energy that Mera hadn't known she possessed. The longer they continued their planning, the longer Mera had to keep it up, and the more it exhausted her.

On top of that, it had been more than a month since they embarked on this mission to discover her family's darkest secret, and her mother was further away than ever.

Mera let Ani and Wyatt continue the discussion of anchors, leaning back against the tree she was sitting under and closing her eyes. She was tired of problems with no solutions. She tried to shift her focus to the sounds of the birds chirping and the wind rustling the tall grass around them, letting Wyatt and Ani's voices fade into the background. It was a warm day for fall. She could wear a T-shirt again, after so many days of layering up against the Maine autumn breeze.

The necklace gave a small jerk and then went white hot. She sat up and reached for it, gasping, and that's when she felt it—a prickling sensation behind her eyes. They filled with tears.

Mera's watery eyes gave her surroundings a distorted, underwater quality. Ani and Wyatt shimmered in front of her as a low buzzing filled her ears. It was like being on a phone call that was consumed by bad reception.

She closed her eyes and shook her head, panic creeping up in her chest. Was she losing control of her powers again? The prickling turned into a pulsing, sending small shockwaves through her brain. The buzzing was growing louder, turning into an indecipherable murmuring. Tears spilled from her eyes, and she cried out in pain, but couldn't hear it.

Hands took her by the shoulders. She knew it was Wyatt in front of her, with Ani hovering nearby, but they just shimmered formlessly.

Mera's eyes locked onto the shape of a tree a few feet away from them. Her senses sharpened, the pulsing growing faster, the murmuring buzz in her head becoming clearer until she realized it was a male voice speaking, his voice quick and low. Behind the tree, the shimmer intensified.

Mera stood, moving toward the tree like it was pulling her there. The closer she got, the more intense the pulsing became. She made out the words in her head. *Did she see me? Do I run?*

She saw a face peek out from behind the trunk. The eyes widened in surprise. *Oh no*, the voice exclaimed, full of fear, *oh no!*

The shimmer sprinted from behind the tree, making for the open forest. The sound of her own voice filled her mind, found the runner dashing away among the trees—

"*Stop!*"

The shimmer came to a sudden halt. Mera took a hesitant step forward as her vision cleared. The leaves crunched underneath her feet, which told her that her hearing had also returned. The shimmering figure in front of her dissolved its glimmering shield until it became a teenage boy.

"Clay," Wyatt said, at her shoulder now.

"What are you doing here?" Ani asked, standing next to Wyatt.

The boy's eyes darted between the three of them.

Did you hear us? Mera asked, her will for him to answer absolute. The question reverberated in his mind. His eyes bulged in terror, locked on Mera.

"Yes," he whispered, his small voice shaking.

"Yes?" Wyatt asked, looking between Mera and Clay. "Yes, what?"

Are you going to turn us in?

This time, Clay nodded, a tear spilling down his cheek.

"Mera, what are you doing?" Wyatt asked, his voice filled with concern as he stared between Mera and his terrified cousin.

Forget what you heard, she commanded. *Forget that you were spying on us. You're going to go home, and you won't remember any of this.*

Clay nodded again, and a desperate confusion seized his features. "What am I doing here? I don't want to be here." More tears spilled down his cheek.

"Then go," Mera said aloud, pointing the way out of the woods.

Clay ran, not looking back once. The farther away he got, the more drained Mera became. She stumbled, catching herself on a nearby tree. She looked up and saw Wyatt and Ani staring at her, wearing identical expressions of shock and something else. Fear.

Mera slid down the tree until she was sitting on the ground again. Wyatt and Ani approached her.

"What did you do?" Wyatt asked, his voice just above a whisper.

Ani answered for her. "You controlled his mind."

"I didn't know you could do that," Wyatt said.

Mera was shaking from her exhaustion, and her voice came out in shudders. "I've never done it before—not exactly."

She wasn't sure how she had done it. Her power had controlled her in that moment—it had sensed a danger nearby and surged into action, equipping her every sense with a weapon. Exactly what Ida had insisted she learn to stop doing.

But Mera was glad for it. If her powers hadn't taken control, they would've been turned into Rochester and facing unknowable consequences before dinner. But she remembered Ida's words.

Bend your powers to your will, not the other way around. The energy must obey you.

Well, Clay had obeyed her powers, and that was good enough for now.

Mera remembered Wyatt's connection to Clay. She looked up at him. "He was going to turn us in. I told him to go home and forget what he saw."

Wyatt considered her for another moment and nodded. "It could've been a lot worse. For all of us."

"We should go. It's getting late," Ani said.

Mera sensed Ani was avoiding looking at her. Wyatt, however, couldn't stop. He moved toward Mera, holding out his hand to help her up. She took it, his warmth seeping into her as soon as their hands made contact. Just touching him made her weariness wane. Once she was on her feet, Wyatt let go, but the gentle flame he had lit inside her remained.

"Thank you," she said to him.

He nodded. They both looked at Ani, who glanced away. The three of them hurried out of the clearing without another word.

NINETEEN

IDA WAS WAITING outside the school at 4:30. Mera worried her grandmother might notice her intense exhaustion, but as she slid into the passenger seat, she was grateful to see Ida was instead preoccupied with staring out the window.

They drove home in silence, and when they pulled up to the house, Ida asked her to meet in the dining room. They would spend their training session this evening focusing on the history of Elemental lore, a history that Ida was adamant Mera learn. Most Elementals were not educated in the "Old Ways," Ida often remarked.

They sat together in the dining room. Ida had just begun her lesson when Mera yawned. She tried to hide it behind her hand, but her grandmother's eyes narrowed.

"Do not take this lightly, Mera," Ida warned.

"Sorry," Mera muttered, sitting up in the seat. "I know this is important."

"The key to an Elemental's power is their connections—to the Element, to themselves, to their community, and to their family. It is the energy of our Element—water—that fuels us. It surrounds us and protects us. Its energy is alive and seeks us out as its equal.

"This is where your inner self becomes important—having the strength of will and courage to meet this energy and match its power with your own. Power without control is not power—it is certain destruction."

Her last words were a punch in Mera's gut. Clay's face, tear-stained and terrified, flashed in her mind. She shook it away, but Ida was staring at her. Had Ida glimpsed the boy's face?

"Certain destruction, got it. What's next?" Mera asked, keeping her voice steady.

Ida looked at her for several beats, then continued.

"The energy will consume you, if you do not learn to control it. But if your strength can match the energy's power —and let me be clear, that requires unyielding diligence and self-restraint," she paused here, staring at her granddaughter, "you will be at peace with it. But as you have learned, we aren't the only beings that draw power from the Elements."

"The Wisps," Mera said.

"The Wisps are one example, but there are many more creatures like them. Not all pose a threat, but some are deadly. It's why Elementals live in communities, despite our differences. A community with the Elements working in harmony provides the strongest protection available to our kind."

"What kind of protection? Like, Rochester?"

Ida looked like she had just swallowed a bug. "I do not mean Rochester. Our collective energies create a natural protective barrier—"

"Oh right, you told me this before. The bubble thing

around the town that keeps out bad stuff."

"Please do not refer to our most ancient and valuable cumulative power as the bubble thing."

"Sorry."

"As I was saying, our protective barrier guards against any being that may wish to do us harm, be that a creature, or . . ." Ida trailed off, her gaze drawn again to the window.

"How did the Wisps get in, then? If our community has this magical protection, how are they in the village?"

"It is not magic, Mera. And if you were listening, you'll know the answer."

"I was listening! You said that when the four Elements come together, our energy makes a non-magical, non-bubble barrier," Mera started thinking out loud. "No, you said in harmony. Well, with the Terras upending the natural order of everything—"

Ida nodded.

"See? I was paying attention."

"Since Rochester and the Terras seized power, our community has been fractured. The barrier has grown weaker and more vulnerable to attack."

Mera's heart sank. What would happen if the barrier vanished? Mera looked out of the window. She imagined innumerable creatures crawling across the front lawn in the dead of night, slinking toward the house. Mera felt Ida access the image, so low were her defenses at this point.

"The Terras have bent and twisted the natural laws to fit the narrative they want us to believe—a narrative that gives them power over the rest of us, that serves the interest of one scared group over the betterment of the whole. Any power they obtain makes us all weaker as a result," Ida's voice was hard. "This makes the last connection so vital."

"Family," Mera said, a knot in her stomach.

Ida's eyes were back at the window.

"Family is one word for it, but perhaps a truer one is ancestry. Heritage. Our blood. That is the root of our abilities. It's what links us to the original source of our powers—to the very first Elementals. Understanding and honoring this connection grounds us."

A tingle in her mind made Mera think about anchors again.

"That connection," Ida continued, "is a source of power that can never leave you. It is more than the physicality of other family members. You did not come into existence as a single entity. You are the product of the energy and efforts of your ancestors, going back thousands of years. That is within you, now and always. The only person who can deny this connection to you is yourself."

A tear slid down Mera's cheek. Ida turned away from her, as though to give her privacy. Mera was so alone without her mother, isolated by the secrets preventing a genuine relationship with Ida.

Mera felt the loneliness lift from her heart as she opened herself to the connection that Ida described. She knew nothing about her ancient ancestors, but she could see her mom's face in her mind.

"It's imperative you honor these connections," Ida said. "They can be the difference between life and death. I need you to understand this, Mera, and always remember—"

Mera stood, her chair clattering to the floor.

"Mera?" Ida exclaimed.

Something was happening, but she couldn't make sense of it. She could hear Ida chastising her in the dining room, but she could also hear the clatter of metal, a loud crack.

She turned to Ida with panic burning inside her chest. Sheriff Rochester had just broken through the gate and was making his way up the drive with five other Terra officers in tow.

Ida sensed it, as well. She sprang from her chair and left the room at a full sprint, leaving Mera to hurry along in her wake. Though she was terrified, Mera couldn't help but admire Ida's agility as she struggled to keep up with her.

Ida reached the front door, and Mera joined her, her necklace dancing on her chest. Rochester and his fellow officers were exiting their cars. They bent their heads together for a moment and then approached the house.

"Upstairs, now," Ida ordered.

"Ida—"

"Do not argue. Go!" Ida said, authority in her voice. She turned to look at Mera, who hesitated, until she spoke again, softer. "Mera, please."

Mera hurried halfway up the stairs, ducking out of sight on the landing. Her heart was pounding, the fear making her muscles stiff. She lowered herself onto shaky knees, peering down at the front door while staying out of sight.

Was it possible that her powers hadn't worked on Clay after all? If he had remembered what happened, he would have gone straight to the Terras to report Mera, Wyatt, and Ani. She thought of her friends—were officers paying a visit to them right now?

Mera's necklace was vibrating, and her mind was spiraling

out of control. She felt the panic pounding inside her, like a prisoner trying to break free.

"Mera," Ida's voice broke into Mera's panic. "Control."

Mera took a deep breath and tried to focus on relaxing. Ida opened the front door.

Ida filled the doorway like a wall, blocking the men from Mera's view. But Mera didn't need to see them; she could feel them. Their energy reminded Mera of having dirt caked under her fingernails.

"Here we are again, Ida," Rochester's voice boomed, as if he were greeting her for dinner.

Rochester was standing in the center, flanked by his officers. His cloak of arrogance only extended so far down the line of his men. Whatever confidence Rochester was projecting, most of the men were terrified of Ida. Mera could sense Ida sharpest of all, churning inside with anger and trepidation, but standing strong in the doorframe, an immovable force. Mera shuddered They were right to be afraid.

"Rochester," Ida responded.

"You mean Sheriff Rochester, Ida. You always seem to forget that. Old age will do that, I suppose," Rochester sneered.

"Ah yes, and it also affords me the privilege of telling you I do not care. What do you want?"

"We're here for your granddaughter," he boomed.

"Why?"

"Because I said so, that's why. Now, where is she?"

"Mrs. Kellen," another officer cut in, "we believe there might have been an incident between your granddaughter and a Terra boy at school, Clay Willoughby. We were looking to ask her a couple of questions."

Mera closed her eyes and focused on her breathing, trying to stem the tide of alarm in her stomach. *Control*, she whispered to herself, *control*.

"Is it typical to require six Terra officers to ask a teenage girl a few questions?" Ida asked.

"Bring the girl here. *Now!*" Rochester's voice echoed through the house.

The air around Ida shimmered, her anger moving closer to the surface.

"Mera is a minor under my care, and you need my permission to speak with her. Permission that I do not grant."

"Permission," Rochester hissed, taking a step closer to Ida, his face now inches from hers. "As if you have ever been able to tell me what I can and can't do."

"Please, Mrs. Kellen," the other officer appealed to Ida again. Mera picked his name from his mind—Patrick. "We found Clay wandering on the side of the road. Didn't have any memory of where he had been before, and all he could say was that he had to go home. It appeared his mind had been . . . tampered with."

Mera's heart clenched. It should have been a relief to learn Clay hadn't turned her in. She had no idea her powers had that effect. Would his mind recover?

"Disoriented. Possessed by a single idea. Minds being tampered with. Sound familiar to you, Ida?" Rochester growled.

A surge of nervous energy escaped the other officers.

"We just need to know where Mera was after school today

—that's the period that Clay can't remember," Patrick interjected.

"It sounds to me like the boy is confused," Ida replied, her voice devoid of emotion. "I hope he was taken to a Salamander for proper care."

Rochester made a loud noise of protest, but Ida continued.

"Mera was in her after-school Homework Club. It meets until four thirty. You can verify with the school."

"Oh, we will. I was on that girl from the moment I saw her. She's not fooling me, and neither are you. And I promise you, we'll be back for the both of you."

"And I can promise you when that day comes, I will not be afraid."

Rochester spat on the porch. "You will learn your place, Kellen. And I will be the one to teach you." He turned and stalked off the porch.

Ida nodded at Patrick then shut the door.

Mera heard the cars take off down the driveway. The next thing she knew, Ida was towering over her.

"Is there anything you'd like to tell me?" Ida asked, steady and quiet.

Mera shook her head. Ida moved by her and up the stairs. Mera stayed on the landing for a long time, the house darkening around her.

TWENTY

PLANNING FOR THE ritual was all but abandoned for the next few weeks as October stretched on. It didn't take long for news of the sheriff's visit to Ida's house to spread around the town.

Rochester set a curfew for the village, decreeing it was now illegal to be out past sunset. Minors required an adult chaperone in public, so no teenagers were allowed out alone. An Elemental's use of their power outside of their home was outlawed. Anyone found in violation of these new laws would be arrested. These extreme regulations, paired with what Rochester was calling a violent attack against Clay, had set the entire village on edge.

Clay was back in school the next day, seemingly unharmed. His memory of those few hours after school never returned, but he made a point to steer clear of Mera every time they passed each other in the hallway. The other teen Terras also kept their distance. Tara would eye her disdainfully but drop her gaze once Mera returned her stare. Watching the Terras hustle away from her should have brought Mera some relief, but instead, it made her stomach clench. They were *afraid* of her.

Rochester came to the school to investigate Mera's alibi of being part of the Homework Club. Ani, the group's founder, was summoned to Mr. Crowley's office to face Rochester's wrath, but Ms. Hughes stepped in to vouch for Ani and the club. Ms. Hughes guaranteed the group's activities were legitimate, claiming to be their faculty mentor. Rochester stormed out of the school in a huff.

"But she didn't even know Homework Club existed," Ani recounted to Mera and Wyatt later. "I mean, would I love for it to be on the extracurricular sign-up sheet in the front office? Yes, of course, who wouldn't—"

"She didn't say why, then?" Wyatt cut in. "Why she covered for us?"

"No," Ani said, shaking her head. "I mean, I guess it's nice to know she's so passionate about homework completion—"

"It has nothing to do with Homework Club," Mera said, a pit in her stomach.

Mera recounted the strange fascination Ms. Hughes seemed to have with her when she first arrived in Convergence. The moment with her necklace and the pass in her office. How Ida distrusted her and put an abrupt end to their counseling sessions.

"There is a general rule for Elementals not to associate with non-Elementals. Part of our whole living-in-secret thing," Wyatt thought aloud. "Maybe that's why Ida objected to it?"

"But wouldn't Ida have told me that? She made it seem like there was some deeper reason she didn't want to say."

"Not only is she not an Elemental, she's from Billings.

How would Ms. Hughes even know to run interference with Rochester?" Ani added.

None of them had an answer. Wyatt shrugged and attributed it to good luck, but the knot in Mera's stomach tightened.

Ms. Hughes hadn't quelled Rochester's suspicions in the slightest, though.

Terra officers swarmed campus. They patrolled areas where students often congregated: the cafeteria, the gymnasium, the outdoor quad.

Mera, Wyatt, and Ani began meeting every afternoon in an empty classroom, completing their homework, while trying to fit in hushed conversations about the ritual between the frequent check-ins by suspicious officers.

"Do you think he heard us?" Wyatt whispered after their most recent pop-in.

They had been discussing anchors. They remained at a complete loss for what this part of the ritual required. Every time they talked about it, Mera felt a small prickle in the deepest recesses of her mind, as if she knew the answer but couldn't access it.

"No," assured Mera, who had dipped into the officer's mind as he took a few smug laps around them before heading back out the door. "He was thinking about how much he loved wearing his uniform."

Mera locked eyes with Ani and felt awash in guilt as Ani's eyes darted to her notebook. Ever since the incident with Clay, Ani had been apprehensive about Mera's use of her powers, though she tried to hide it. A few weeks ago, Ani was ecstatic at the idea of seeing an Undine's power, but Ani's mind was her most prized possession. That Mera could infiltrate it, manipulate it—Ani was frightened. Mera wanted to tell Ani that she would never use her powers against her, but could she promise that, when they both knew Mera wasn't always in control of it? Ani was right to be anxious. Mera was, too.

"Cool," Wyatt nodded and looked back at his own notebook. Wyatt viewed her powers as an asset. He often urged her to be on the telepathic lookout for intruders.

Mera retrieved the diary she had hidden when the officer entered. Mera reread the sentence they had been discussing: *Made of time, blood is at once past, present, and future.*

There was that prickle again. An image of Ida sitting at the dining room table flashed in her mind. Telling her something . . . something about blood. Heritage. Ancestry.

"It's me. I'm the anchor."

Wyatt and Ani looked up.

"What?" they both said.

"The connection to the past—to Ida and Darcy—it's me, my blood. And I'm living now, in the present moment. Isn't that what we need? An anchor to the present with a connection to the past?"

"Yes!" Ani cried. "You're right! I mean, at least, you sound right!"

Ani and Mera both looked at Wyatt.

"A thunderstorm," he whispered.

"Okay, well, I don't see how a storm could be the anchor," Ani began, but Wyatt shook his head.

"No, Mera's the anchor. But the other thing we haven't been able to figure out. The disturbance?"

"'One can only look into the past through a great disturbance of the ritual place.'" Mera quoted from the diary.

"That's genius, Wyatt! Of course!" Ani exclaimed, standing up and pacing around. "A thunderstorm is essentially two separate energies colliding!"

Mera seized her notebook and scribbled down their newest ideas, thrilled at their sudden breakthroughs. But when she looked up, she saw Ani had frozen in place.

"Ani," Wyatt prodded, "you okay?"

"Okay, wow," Ani whispered, her eyes the size of saucers. "Great ideas must come in threes, because I just had my own like, epiphany!"

Ani turned on her heel and sprinted from the classroom.

Wyatt and Mera looked at one another for a moment, Mera's confusion mirrored on Wyatt's face. After scrambling to pack the hidden diaries, they hopped up to run after her. They chased her through the deserted hallways, peering around corners to make sure they weren't about to run into any Terras.

When they caught up to Ani, she was standing in front of a large, faded map of the village pinned up on a bulletin board. As Mera and Wyatt approached, panting, Ani pointed at one of the far corners, where the blue of the sea engulfed the edges of the map.

"Your house, Mera," she said in an excited whisper. "Your house is surrounded by the four Elements. We could do the ritual there."

It was right there on the map. The forest on one side, the other open to the air and sun, with the sea below. Mera reached out to touch the cliff where she knew her grandmother's house to be. If Mera wanted to see back to the past and find the truth about her family's history, it would have to be here.

"What about Ida? She never leaves the house. She would probably notice us doing an ancient, powerful ritual in the yard in the middle of a thunderstorm."

"There's a beach below the cliff, right?" Wyatt looked at Ani. "Would that work?"

"Yes! It would! And the energy of the storm should give us all the protection we need!"

A chill went through Mera. She had never been down to the beach. She had no interest after seeing that dark patch in the water when she first arrived. The heavy feeling it gave her, the unconscious step she had taken closer to the cliff, Ida's warning—Mera shivered again and looked up to see Wyatt and Ani staring at her.

"Mera?" Ani asked.

She looked between them. They had worked so hard, putting themselves in danger to help Mera get the information she needed to find her mom. Here they were, ready to do the most perilous thing they could with their combined powers, so what could Mera say to them? She was too afraid of the ocean?

"The beach it is," she said, forcing herself to smile.

Ani jumped up and down. "Okay, then we just need to be on the lookout for the next powerful storm."

"And the Terra object," Wyatt reminded them.

"Oh yes, I had forgotten about that! Well—"

"Can we figure this last piece out next time? I have to meet Ida."

"Yeah, I have to go, too," Wyatt said.

They walked back to the classroom, still careful to check for any unwanted company. Mera tried to shake her uneasiness about the beach. The dark spot in the water hung over her like a shadow.

"So where are you hurrying off to, anyway?" Ani asked Wyatt as they packed up their belongings in the classroom.

"I have to meet my dad at the jeweler downtown before they close. He's having a ring resized for my mom for their anniversary," Wyatt said.

Ani straightened up, focusing on something in the air.

"I have to go!" Ani yelled, picking up her bag and running from the classroom once more.

"This is not what I expected Homework Club to be like," Wyatt said, shaking his head.

***

That night, Mera was excited when Ida told her they would be moving on in her lessons and practicing a defensive technique called shielding. Mera recognized it as being like what Wyatt had projected that day when Tara tried to attack her.

"You allow your power to build, then force it out in all directions, creating a protective shield around yourself," Ida explained.

Pooling her energy, collecting it inside her, was a strange sensation at first. It was chaotic, churning, and Mera would release it too early, her shield evaporating as it met the air.

"Control," Ida reminded.

Mera scowled at her but closed her eyes to concentrate. She let the energy gather in her core, drawing in slow, even breaths to steady herself and the swelling energy inside her. Mera drew it up like a rising tide, steady and relentless, until she was brimming with it. She took a final calming breath, opened her eyes, and pushed the energy out and all around her. It rolled out like a tidal wave and shimmered before she let it go, falling to one knee as the shield disappeared.

"Lovely," Ida said. "Now stand up. Again."

When Mera could reproduce it several times in a row, Ida sent bursts of energy at her. Small at first, the waves of energy nudged Mera when she didn't form her shield in time.

But as her shields improved, so did the intensity of energy coming from Ida, forcing Mera to draw larger amounts of energy to protect herself. The more effective the shield, the more tired Mera became. But Ida didn't let her rest.

"Is this a training session, or are you trying to send me some kind of message?" Mera panted, her heart hammering from exertion.

In response, Ida sent yet another burst of energy. Mera threw up her shield, but the force of Ida's blast sent her tumbling backward.

"Again, Mera," Ida demanded as Mera scrambled to her feet.

"Ida, can we please—"

But Ida sent another wave of energy hurtling toward her. Mera tried to summon the shield, but it died before the energy reached her. It hit her in the stomach and doubled her over.

"Again!" Ida called.

Mera lay on the ground, gasping for breath.

"Up, please."

Mera lifted her head. "No," she stated, letting her head

drop back on the earth.

"We are not finished."

"You may not be, but I am."

"Mera, this is childish."

"It really is, but I'm not getting up until you go back into the house."

Ida let out a sigh and swept from the spot. Mera heard the front door slam a moment later. She lay on the cool grass as twilight set over the lawn. When stars twinkled to life above her, she forced herself to go into the house. Ida was nowhere to be found.

Mera made her way to her room. She slumped at her desk, pulling her books out of her bag, a long evening of homework ahead of her thanks to their productive non-homework Homework Club meeting. But the words in her history textbook were swimming off the page as she tried to focus on them, drawing her thoughts once again to the daunting task before her: the ritual.

Filled with worry, she thought she would rest on her desk for a moment to refocus her thoughts, but she was asleep by the time her head hit her arms.

TWENTY-ONE

MERA WAS IN the middle of the raging ocean. She thrashed and kicked to stay afloat as a hard rain fell on her face. She tried to look around, but the waves were too tall.

The water felt like knives on her skin, the cold finding the heat in her body and forcing it out of her. The chill ran all the way to her bones. She struggled to keep her head above the surface as the waves crashed down on her, the ocean in turmoil from the storm.

A flash of lightning pierced the sky, illuminating the churning water around her in a haunting blue hue. In the bright relief, she saw a figure floating just ahead of her.

"Mom!" Mera screamed, saltwater filling her throat. She gagged and sputtered, her throat burning. She tried to swim forward, but the waves were like a wall, pressing her from all sides, keeping her in place while carrying her mother further away from her. Mera pushed her body through the water, fighting the ocean. With a great effort, Mera was close enough to touch her mother's shoulder.

"Mom, it's me!"

But as her hand connected with her mother's shoulder, the

walls of water formed around her again, keeping her in place. Mera watched in horror as the figure turned toward her. She found herself face to face with a decaying corpse.

Half skeleton, the corpse was a repellent mixture of bones and muscle. The figure's face was a skeleton, covered in a thin layer of green, serrated skin. Its eyes were gone, but its dark sockets bored into Mera. It smiled, its shredded lips peeling away to reveal rotten black fangs. Mera's mouth opened to scream but no sound could escape, saltwater splashing up her nose and down her throat.

A high-pitched laugh filled her mind, raspy but filled with glee.

The corpse's rotted hand shot out and gripped Mera's wrist before diving underwater, dragging Mera with it.

Mera awoke in her bedroom, choking on air. She stood and pushed herself up and away from her desk, her chair tipping over behind her with a dull thud.

Mera clutched the necklace. It was burning white hot, as though ready for a fight. She closed her eyes and gripped it, allowing its warmth to course through her. It pushed the horrifying images from her mind—the waves, the rain, the freezing touch of the corpse. Mera shivered, a chill that wracked her entire body.

She listened but didn't hear Ida stirring in the house. She must not have heard the chair or sensed Mera's fright. Mera sank onto her bed, the room around her coming to life in the pre-dawn glow.

When her heartbeat slowed, Mera knew she wouldn't be able to get back to sleep. Seeing one of her notebooks on the ground, she reached to pick it up and gasped as a bright shock of pain flashed up her wrist. She looked down, and the air rushed out of her lungs.

Around her wrist was a deep, purple-black bruise, right where the corpse's hand had gripped her.

***

The next few days passed for Mera in a haze. She couldn't sleep. Whenever she closed her eyes, the corpse pulled her back under the raging ocean. Every night, she lay awake, drowning in her own anxiety instead.

In the daytime, everything blurred together. Mera marked the passage of time by the flowering of the bruise on her wrist —by Wednesday, it had turned a velvety blue, and she had to layer several bracelets to cover its reach up her arm. She often pushed two of the bracelets aside and examined it during her classes, at lunch with Ani and Wyatt, on the car rides to and from school with Ida.

Had she gripped her own wrist while she slept? Banged it on something?

Her friends grew annoyed with her faraway expression as they continued to plan the ritual. On Thursday, they huddled in the library before homeroom after Ani's insistence that they meet for an "important update." The concern that Wyatt and Ani had displayed at the beginning of the week for Mera's distractedness had waned. Ani had begun snapping her fingers in front of Mera's face, jarring Mera back to reality with an irritating cracking sound.

"Sorry," she murmured. "I'm listening."

"As I was saying," Ani said, sitting up straighter. Her expression of irritation disappeared, and a mischievous grin broke out over her face. "We now have one less thing to worry about."

Mera shook her head, trying to clear the fog that had settled over her brain. She didn't like Ani's expression. She glanced at Wyatt, who was looking apprehensive.

"Is anyone watching?" Ani asked Mera, her smile widening.

Mera liked this even less. Ani asking her to use her powers? She forced herself to focus. She scanned the room with her mind.

"All clear," she said.

Ani reached into her bag and took out a velvet purple pouch. She reached inside and pulled out a crystal-clear uncut diamond larger than a baseball.

"One powerful Terra object, check! It's the last thing we need for the ritual!" Ani chirped. She looked around at Wyatt and Mera, and her smile faltered. "Um, you're welcome!"

"How did you—" Wyatt began.

"Oh, it was easy! Last week you mentioned the jeweler, and then I remembered! The Rochesters have this collection of precious stones they've been passing down since forever. Each one is like, sacred and special or whatever. Honestly, I don't really remember the specifics, but they're all meant to boost a Terra's power! Isn't that so perfect?"

"I always thought the Rochester family stones thing was made up," Wyatt said, shaking his head. "How did you know where to find them?"

Ani's cheeks flushed "Does that matter?"

"Ani, what were you thinking?" Mera exclaimed. The fog swirling in her skull thickened into anger, taking hold of her mind with heavy tentacles.

Ani blinked a few times. "Wait, you're like, mad?"

"You stole a diamond from Rochester," Mera hissed.

"Okay, yes, on paper, doesn't sound great, but—" Wyatt attempted.

"I didn't steal it, it's borrowed. And I was really careful—"

"Ani," Mera cut in. "Rochester is already so suspicious. What do you think he's going to do when he finds an ancient diamond missing from his own home? You need to bring it back. Now."

"There's a big storm coming tomorrow." Ani pulled a newspaper from her bag and tossed it onto the table. It was folded back to the weather page, and the small box for Friday showed dark gray clouds with lightning bolts and rain. "There's no time to find another Terra object this powerful before then."

"Ani, can you live in reality for once?" Mera snapped through clenched teeth. "How can someone so smart do something so stupid?"

The words were foreign in her brain, and she regretted saying them. Wyatt gaped at her, but Ani's expression set in defiance.

"Just because you can't control your powers doesn't mean that all of ours are too dangerous to use," Ani retorted before standing and storming out of the library.

TWENTY-TWO

MERA BOLTED UPRIGHT in bed. She looked around, sunlight streaming through the curtains.

There was a creak in the hallway. A figure breezed by her door.

"You awake, Mer-bear?" her mother called. "Come say bye before I leave for work."

"Mom?" Mera's voice cracked with relief.

She scrambled off her bed and made for the door. Her eyes blurred with tears as she moved down the hallway, chasing after her mother. Mera could only see her long, dark hair vanishing around corners.

"I have to go," her mom said, gathering up her things. "If I'm late, Darcy'll kill me."

Wait. A ringing sound clouded Mera's mind.

"No, Mom! Don't go!" Mera cried, racing down the stairs. As she reached the bottom, she waded into the surf on the beach. She stopped, the waves lapping around her knees.

Her mom was in front of her, her back to Mera.

"Mera, what is it?" her mom called.

The water continued to push and pull at Mera's legs,

moving up her body higher and higher, swirling and cinching around her like a vise. Her mother turned, and Mera gasped. The woman's face was so like Mera's mother, but the features were sharper, the hair bright white. The water was at Mera's neck.

"Now take a deep breath, my love. You're going to need it," Darcy said. Her ruined, decayed hand grabbed Mera by the hair and pulled her into the frigid waves.

Mera's eyes flew open as the sound of shattering glass exploded around her. The necklace burned against her chest, wisps of smoke rising as it seared a hole in her T-shirt.

Ida burst into the bedroom, sending the glass fragments on the floor flying against the far bedroom wall, ready to attack.

"What happened?"

Mera struggled to sit. Her ears rang, just as in the dream. Mera blinked a few times and tried to bring the scene in her bedroom into focus. Cold night air was gushing into the room through the broken windows. Shattered glass littered the floor.

"I'm sorry," Mera said, pressing her shaking hands against her ears. The ringing. "I'll help you replace them."

"The windows are not my concern."

The two stared at each other. Mera's heartbeat was slowing down, though the intensity of ringing persisted. Ida sat on the bed.

"I didn't feel any of your fear, or your panic, Mera," Ida said, turning to look her granddaughter in the eye. "What exactly happened? You were dreaming?"

Tell her nothing, a voice in Mera's mind spoke. *She'll never give you what you need, only stop you from getting it.*

"What happened, Mera?" Ida asked again, a note of pleading in her voice.

"If you tell me your dream, I'll tell you mine," Mera heard herself respond.

Ida looked at her in shock. Mera's face burned red. She turned away from Ida, surprised by the venom in her words.

"I see," Ida said. She stood. "You can stay in the guest room. I'll replace the windows tomorrow."

She left Mera to gather her things and hobble into the closest guest bedroom.

Mera dropped into a soft recliner chair by the window. A deep ache filled her chest and reached out into the rest of her body, tears blurring her vision of the sun coming up over the horizon.

***

Ida and Mera emerged on the landing at the same time the next morning. They ate breakfast and drove to school in silence, which suited Mera. The ringing in her ears had only gotten worse. It became so loud sometimes that it vibrated her teeth, and she could hear nothing else but its piercing drone.

Mera moved through her entire day as if she were underwater. She floated through the packed hallways, the volume of her classmates muted and distant. She avoided Ani and Wyatt by arriving just before the bell to each of her classes and then losing herself in the hallway's riptide as soon as class ended.

Mera skipped the library for lunch and planted herself in the back corner of the cafeteria. Wyatt and Ani came marching up to her within a few minutes of the lunch bell.

"I thought we were meeting in the library?" Wyatt asked,

throwing his bag on the table.

"Mera, about yesterday," Ani began, taking a seat next to Mera. "I'm sorry. I just got caught up in the excitement about the ritual."

Oh, so she's having fun, the voice in Mera's mind spoke again. *Like it's a game.*

"Excitement is one word for it, I guess," Mera mumbled.

"Oh, I didn't mean excitement like, yay excitement, I just —" Ani stumbled over her words then looked at Wyatt for help.

"We know how tough it's been," Wyatt jumped in.

Oh, they're a "we" now? the voice questioned.

"Especially for you, Mera," Ani added.

So they're a "we" and you're a "you." Always the outsider, no matter how hard you try . . .

"What does that mean?" Mera strained to keep her voice measured.

Ani's eyes widened in panic. She looked again at Wyatt. Why did she keep looking at him?

"Everything you've been through," Wyatt answered for Ani. "Your family situation—"

"Oh, right. Please tell me more about my family situation, like I'm not the one living it."

"What? No, I—"

Mera knew it was unfair, but the ringing was in her spine now, traveling down her back, into her legs. Exhaustion swept over her again.

"Mera, are you okay?" Ani asked, the desperation creeping into her voice.

"I'm fine."

Wyatt and Ani exchanged a look, and Mera's irritation flared.

"Mera . . ." Wyatt began, pulling himself close to the table. He leaned in and stared at her.

Mera wasn't sure if he was meaning to send his waves of concern washing over her, or if it was pouring out of him in the same way Mera had trouble controlling her energy when she was overwhelmed. His warmth broke through the fog in her mind, and the necklace warmed against her chest. She wanted nothing more than to confide in her friends, let their support revive her as Wyatt's energy had, let them stand watch over her while she put her head down on the table and slept, safe.

"What's wrong?" Wyatt whispered, his energy soothing the jagged edges in her mind.

This must be Plan B. He'll get you to talk, one way or another . . . the voice returned.

Mera thought of Ani's insult the day before, about Mera being unable to control her powers. Wyatt had more control over his powers than her.

He's doing this on purpose to set you at ease, to trick you into trusting him.

Mera remembered the other times she had felt him do this. Ever since they met, was he just using his powers to manipulate her? To get close to her? But *why*? She pulled back from the warmth passing between them with such abrupt force that it felt like someone had doused her with ice water. Wyatt recoiled as the wave of cold traveled out from her, and Ani let out a gasp and shivered.

She kept her eyes down. She couldn't bear to see the

unspoken fear that passed between them.

"There's nothing wrong," Mera tried again, pushing the ringing to the back of her mind. What was the matter with her? She knew they were only trying to help. Weren't they? "Thanks, you know . . . for asking." The voice in her mind grumbled with disapproval.

"Well," Ani began after a few uncomfortable moments. "The storm is supposed to hit late tonight. We should meet at the beach at ten, before it starts, to set up."

Mera thought of the darkened beach in her nightmare and her hair stood on end. She shuddered, lost in the moment, almost tasting the salty ocean air.

"Okay," Wyatt said, his attempt at cheer less convincing than Ani's. "Do we need to go over things one more time?"

"No," Mera blurted. Ani deflated beside her.

"Are you sure?" Ani said, her eyes fluttering up to meet Mera's. "I mean, we all know what we're doing then?"

Still doesn't believe you're up to the task. And you think these two are your friends?

Resentment surged in Mera. No wonder she couldn't bring herself to tell either of them the truth. With Wyatt using his powers on her and Ani's constant doubt, they clearly didn't trust her either.

"All set. See you tonight," Mera said suddenly, standing and reaching for her backpack. Mera's head was heavy, and she swayed on the spot.

Wyatt reached out to steady her, but Mera backed away from his touch.

Swinging her backpack onto her shoulder, Mera walked away from them.

TWENTY-THREE

A FULL AFTERNOON spent avoiding Ani and Wyatt and another silent car ride home with Ida gave Mera plenty of time to stew in her own misery.

During dinner, the silence between them amplified the hum in her ears, sending shooting pains from her head to her feet.

"Thank you for replacing my windows and cleaning everything up," Mera said, desperate to fill the void of sound.

Ida continued eating without a reply.

"Maybe you could show me how to do that. Fixing windows and stuff," Mera continued.

"If you worked harder to control your powers, things wouldn't need fixing as often."

"I am trying."

But Ida said nothing.

Nothing is ever good enough, is it? the voice chided.

Mera stared at Ida, a tide of bitter anger rising inside her.

She was tired of Ida's silence. More than that, she was tired of Ida's lack of interest in Mera's existence.

Maybe she'd prefer you disappeared, too. . . .

Mera slammed down her fork and pushed her chair back

from the table. Ida didn't even look up from her plate. Mera stormed upstairs, tempted to destroy everything she passed out of spite.

***

Ida retired to her study after dinner, so it was easy for Mera to descend the staircase undetected in the dark. She paused at the foot of the stairs, thinking she heard a man's voice from the closed door of the study. After casting her senses out, Mera felt only Ida in the house.

Mera slipped onto the porch and saw Wyatt and Ani silhouetted in the moonlight, walking up the driveway and speaking in hushed tones. A fist clenched in Mera's stomach.

Hmm, wonder who—I mean what—they're talking about?

"Mera!" Ani exclaimed when she saw her, but both Wyatt and Mera shushed her. Mera pointed toward the path that led to the cliffs, and the three of them hurried away from the house.

When they were far enough down the path, Ani tried again. "Um. What's up? And don't say nothing, okay?"

Mera wheeled around, avoiding her friends' eyes.

"I'm fine."

"Well, I'm not," Wyatt said, crossing his arms. "I don't think we should do the ritual."

"What? Why?" Mera gasped.

"You're not yourself."

"Oh, like you're some kind of authority on that subject?" Mera snapped. "Look, I'm tired. But I'm okay."

Mera needed them to go through with the ritual. She needed answers about her family, and she needed them tonight. She couldn't go back to that house, filled with Ida's

184

silence and secrets.

Thunder rolled in the distance, and the first drops of rain fell from the sky, padding along the path like carpeted footsteps.

"Ani?" Mera turned to Ani, who was chewing her lip and looking at Wyatt.

"I know how important this is to you, but . . . you've seemed like, off lately. And for this ritual, we all have to be, you know, on."

Fear that her friends would abandon her rose in Mera's chest, and panic clouded her foggy mind.

You could help them make the right choice, the voice whispered as a familiar tingle spread in her mind. *I'm sure your mother will understand, wherever she is. . . .*

Mera forced herself to look up at Wyatt's face, desperate to find that part of him again that was so comforting.

"This doesn't feel right," Wyatt said, his arms still crossed over his chest. "There's something you aren't telling us."

If they were your friends, why would they stand in the way of finding your poor mother?

The tingling at the edge of her mind was pounding now. The rain had picked up. As it fell onto Mera, the drops mixed with her tears as they flowed down her cheeks.

If you want to save your mother, you know what you have to do. It's the only way. . . .

"I'm sorry," Mera heard herself whisper.

"Mera," Wyatt said, taking a step closer.

Mera locked eyes with him. The tingling released and moved toward him like a magnet, her power entering Wyatt's mind.

"*I haven't been sleeping,*" Mera said aloud, in a faraway voice. "*I've been having nightmares. But I'm okay, I promise. We've come this far, and we need to see this through.*"

Guided by her power, Mera's words sought Wyatt's misgivings and overwrote them. Wyatt's resistance fell away as Mera's will replaced his concern with false assurances.

"Okay," Wyatt sighed, uncrossing his arms. "If you're sure."

"Oh, Mera, I'm so sorry! That sounds awful! Thank you for telling us," Ani rushed forward and pulled Mera into a tight hug. Mera tried to control her grimace as Ani stepped back again. "If we're going to do the ritual, we should head down to the beach—the storm is almost here."

Ani glanced at Wyatt, who nodded and gave Mera a small smile.

Something broke within her, something deep and precious that could never be restored. The voice was laughing in her mind, and she had to shake her head to clear it.

***

The beach was rocky and wild. No one had been there in years. The waves were roiling from the storm. The water was slick like oil, and lightning cracked in the sky. There was a strong smell of something rotten. Her sense of foreboding was increasing as the thunder roared.

Ani shrugged her backpack off. She pulled out supplies and handed them around, first a tarp and rope, then folded up tent poles.

They began setting up the tarp halfway down the beach in a clearing on the sand, yelling directions at one another over the sound of the angry surf. Wind whipped around as the storm barreled toward them over the sea, the billowing gray-black clouds churning ever closer. The stakes sank with ease into the damp sand and held the shelter in place. They hurried into the makeshift tent.

"Ugh," Mera gagged as they settled themselves. "That smell."

"What smell?" Wyatt asked, handing Ani her bag and arranging a flashlight so they could see one another in the dark.

"You don't smell that?"

"I don't smell anything," Ani said as she dug in her bag.

Mera shook her head. There wasn't time to discuss it.

"Never mind, let's just get ready. The storm's almost here."

The three busied themselves with setting up their makeshift tent as the wind whipped against it, but they stayed dry.

"Seriously, great idea with the tarp, Ani," Mera said, offering her a weak smile.

"And the lights," Wyatt said as Ani withdrew two battery powered lanterns from her bottomless backpack.

"Thanks," Ani said, grinning as she set up the lanterns in the small space between them.

The roaring of the storm outside drowned out the buzzing in her mind, and Mera felt more clearheaded than she had in days, her adrenaline pumping.

Ani removed the last item from her backpack and placed it in the center of them. The Terra diamond glinted like a prism in the lantern light.

"Who brought the bowl for the uh—the anchor?" Ani asked, shooting nervous glances at Mera.

Wyatt produced a small silver bowl from his jacket pocket.

A sharp clap of thunder sent a jolt through the beach, and Wyatt's hand shook a little as he placed the bowl next to the diamond. From his other pocket he took a faded Swiss army knife.

Mera took the knife, and before she could think better of it, she sliced open her fingertip. The blood dripped from the wound, and she leaned forward to let it fall into the bowl.

"Do you think that's good?" Mera asked, withdrawing her hand and cradling the cut on her finger.

Ani was sheet white, staring at the blood pooled in the silver bowl.

"It's going to have to be," Wyatt said, reaching out his hand.

Mera handed him the knife, but he reached again for her injured finger. Without a word, he enveloped her hand in his. There was a moment of warmth before he withdrew his hand. The warmth was gone, but so was the wound. Mera looked up at him.

"Thank you," Mera's eyes traveled up to his and lingered for a moment. Then, she remembered the broken thing inside of her and tore her eyes away. She had made her choice, after all.

"We have to write the date and the place we want to . . . is *visit* the right word?" Ani said. "And then we put it in the— ugh, I'm sorry, it's so gross—the anchor."

"You mean the blood bowl?" Wyatt said.

Ani closed her eyes, looking queasy. "Yes," she confirmed.

"Here, I brought my notebook," Mera said, and she produced a pad and pen for Ani.

Ani wrote the date and place of Ida and Darcy's infamous

showdown, tore it from the pad, and pressed it onto the drops of blood in the bowl. The crimson bled through the white paper.

Another flash of lightning illuminated the beach in front of them, and Mera gasped. In the relief, she thought she had seen a figure standing in the water. She shook her head. No one would be in the water right now. No one could be.

"All right," Ani said, looking at Wyatt and Mera. "It's time. Wyatt, move closer. Now, we have to focus all of our collective energy on our objective—seeing the battle. We have to work as one."

Ani extended her hands, and Wyatt and Mera did the same. They all closed their eyes.

With every ounce of effort, Mera let the sounds of the rain, the roar of the turbulent ocean, and the rumble of the storm fall away. She focused on the day that Ida and Darcy had their faceoff, playing her memory of Ida's dream like a record in her mind, the needle dancing on and off.

Mera felt a prickling in her hands. It took her a moment to realize that the vibrations in her fingertips were coming from Wyatt and Ani, their energy searching for hers.

Their energies were distinct. Ani's was cool and light, gathering briefly around each person and object before moving again, curious and swift. Wyatt's was heavier and warm. It remained still, growing in its intensity and flickering like a pulse.

With another deep breath, she let her energy flow out through her fingertips. Hers alternated between hot and cold, moving from place to place like a current, gathering power as it circled and filled. Her energy connected with Wyatt and

Ani's with a slight but satisfying hum, and the warm sensation in her core surged.

Prodded by the energy of the other three Elements, the Terra diamond came alive. Its energy was muted, grounded, and sturdy. The diamond smoothed out their energies, settling and uniting them.

The energies, working as one now, swirled around the bowl, slowly at first and then faster and faster. The paper caught fire as the blood churned. Then, as though a plug had been pulled at the base of the bowl, the whirlpool drained. Mera gasped as their collective energy was pulled into the void along with the ash and blood, back to the past.

TWENTY-FOUR

WHEN MERA OPENED her eyes, she was standing in a moonlit clearing clouded by fog and smoke.

The Convergence, she thought, looking around her. Beside her stood Wyatt and Ani, although Mera could barely make them out, even in the moonlight's glow. She held out her arm and saw that she was semi-transparent. Mera tried to call out to them but found she had no voice. She saw Ani clutching her own translucent throat with a look of surprise. Wyatt just shook his head. Only their energy had traveled here—they had left their corporeal bodies in the present. They were ghosts from the future, invisible in the past.

Mera looked down and opened her mouth to form the specter of a scream. On the ground was the body of a woman, her eyes open, her face fixed in terror. The woman's skin was blue, her eyes bloodshot, but she had no apparent wounds. She just looked . . . empty.

There were bodies strewn all over the clearing, their blind eyes glittering in the haunted moonlight.

Ani had her hand over her eyes. Wyatt's was over his mouth.

This field of the dead wasn't in Ida's dream. It was a detail that Ida's mind had spared her.

The body of a middle-aged man a few steps ahead of them stirred. He clutched his hand to his chest with a gasp of breath that rattled across the silent field.

The thick fog in the clearing parted on a breeze, and Mera saw his eyes widen in terror.

"Please, Darcy. Please no more," the man whispered.

Darcy. A jolt shot through Mera. She turned to see a shadowy figure standing in a revolving cloud of smoke and fog.

"They're all dead," the man said in a small voice, pulling himself to his knees. "It's over."

Darcy took a step forward, consuming the fog as she moved, visible now in the unobstructed moonlight.

Mera's breathing quickened as she took in Darcy for the first time.

Darcy was tall like Ida but stick thin where her sister was solid. She would have looked delicate in her long, lace dress if it weren't for the power emanating from her. Her white hair was tied into a high, clean bun, and her gray eyes glowed in the darkness as her pale skin shone blue.

"It's over, Rochester," Darcy said, drawing ever closer.

Mera, Ani, and Wyatt started all at once.

Rochester's father, Ani mouthed, pointing at the man on the ground.

"For you," Darcy snarled.

Rochester closed his eyes and let out a gasp, as the undulating energy around Darcy expanded and arced, ready to strike.

Just before it engulfed Rochester, a familiar voice commanded, "Stop!"

Mera's heart soared as Ida strode through the clearing, blasting a way for herself through Darcy's fog. Ida was more fearsome than Mera had ever seen her, her face a mask of determination. She looked younger, of course, but just as serious, her features sharpened in concentration as she glared so fiercely at her sister that Mera felt herself shrinking back from her. But Darcy did not move.

"I told you to leave," Darcy said, her voice deep and commanding.

"And I said no. Enough, Darcy."

"I am not done."

Even in her ghostlike state, phantom crackles of energy prickled Mera's skin as Darcy and Ida squared off. A sudden clap of thunder shook the ground.

"They're dead!" Ida's face was wet with tears, and her hands shook at her side. A flash of lightning cut through the sky.

"Not all of them! Not Rochester, not the cowards who ran. They should get away with what they did?"

Mera looked at the bodies on the ground again, aware that Darcy must have already killed the rest of their family. *Our family*, Mera corrected herself.

"Darcy, please."

"We're past that, Ida. You think you have the power to stop me?"

"It's not just about power."

Another roll of thunder. Another arc of lightning.

The sky unleashed a downpour, but the sisters were

impervious to the rain. Their energies expanded and curved around them like shields.

"You've broken every law of nature and the laws of our community. You may have the power you took, but you have become untethered."

"Enough of the bedtime stories! I'm building a new future, and no one will stand in my way. Not even you."

A bolt of lightning ripped through the clouds, and the sisters surged forward.

Their two energy fields met with a loud crack. The wave of the connection sent Mera, Wyatt, and Ani flying backward. The ground rumbled beneath them, catching fire and freezing.

Mera struggled back to her feet. She looked around, but Wyatt and Ani were nowhere to be seen. Mera didn't have long to search for her friends, as another wave of energy from the battle hit her square in the chest. She hit the ground hard, losing her breath. The rain was coming down on her face, stinging her eyes.

But no, that wasn't right. She was a ghost here. Mera held up her hand and watched the rain splash against her skin.

A roll of thunder shook the ground beneath her as she stood and hobbled forward. Fog obscured the sisters, and Mera had to shield her eyes to keep the rain from blinding her.

There was a strangled cry from within the cloud, and then a blast of warm air parted it. Before Mera was the scene from Ida's dream—Ida standing over Darcy, her energy bearing down on her sister. A tearful Darcy raised her hands, struggling to hold Ida at bay.

"Please," Darcy begged. "Ida—"

"The time for mercy has passed, Darcy."

"Think of Genevieve," Darcy pleaded. "What will happen to her?"

"That is the only thing I'm thinking about," Ida said.

Ida pulled back her hands to build one last surge of power that rippled in the moonlight, then brought them down again, aimed at Darcy's heart. Darcy screamed, a terrible, heartbreaking wail.

The rain stopped just as suddenly as it had begun. Ida stood back from her sister. Darcy stirred on the ground, crying and panting.

Darcy was alive.

Darcy panted as she stared up at Ida. Ida staggered back a few paces, her own breathing shallow and labored.

Mera felt herself being jerked by the shoulders. She heard Wyatt and Ani in the distance, calling her name. But she couldn't leave. Not yet.

"What have you done to me?" Darcy screeched.

Ida's face was inscrutable.

Mera, her mother's voice cut across her mind as if over a loudspeaker.

It's coming! she screamed.

Mera fell to her knees, clutching her head. She heard screams and shouting in the distance, and the rotting smell filled her nostrils. Wyatt and Ani were in trouble.

Mera looked up and found that the scene at the Convergence had changed. Ida, Darcy, and the field of bodies had vanished. Her mother was standing over her, fear etched in every line of her face.

"*Mera, it's here,*" Genevieve whispered, reaching her hand

out for Mera to take.

TWENTY-FIVE

IN THE NEXT instant, Mera was on the beach, the rain falling on her in sheets.

The tarp was gone. The lanterns glowed in the sand, but Wyatt and Ani were nowhere in sight. Mera stood, her knees threatening to give out. Her necklace was on fire, the rain sizzling as it made contact. She gagged—the stench of decay overpowering her.

"Wyatt! Ani!" Mera called, trying to scream over the rain and the crash of the waves.

She closed her eyes and cast out her senses for them. They were close. Mera squinted through the downpour and saw two figures lying in the sand near the water. She ran to them.

Wyatt and Ani were unconscious, the tide at their ankles and advancing fast. Mera held out her hands, and with her power, pulled their bodies to safety up the beach. Ani stirred as Mera dropped down next to her.

"What happened?"

Ani's eyes fluttered open. "In the water," she murmured.

"What?" Mera asked, turning to the ocean.

A flash of lightning lit up the water, and Mera saw the

figure of a woman floating.

Your mother, said the voice in her head. *She came to find you.*

Mera stood and started toward the water.

"Mom?"

"Mera, no!" Ani called from behind her, but Mera did not stop.

She's not your friend, remember? You made your choice.

Mera waded out up to her knees. Her necklace jolted against her chest, but Mera continued to crash into the waves and swam toward the floating body. The sea battled back against her, but Mera fought with her remaining strength.

Be with your mother, Mera.

Mera, it's a Draugr! Ani's voice breezed through her mind. *What you're seeing isn't real.*

A Draugr? Mera didn't understand.

Keep going, Mera. Just a little farther, the voice beckoned.

Mera glimpsed the floating figure. It was within arm's reach now. But Mera stopped, the stormy water rocking her back and forth.

A Draugr is an Undine creature, Ani's voice cut into her mind again. *It stalks its prey—gets into their head. Be careful, Mera, it's probably deep in your mind already. Don't believe what it shows you!*

Mera remembered her dream. What happened when she reached out and touched the figure? It turned out to be—

"The Draugr," Mera said aloud, water filling her mouth. She turned to swim to shore and found herself staring into a rotting, skeletal face.

Hello, Mera, the Draugr spoke into her mind, its ruined

mouth breaking into a sickly smile. Paralyzed, Mera watched as the Draugr forced her under the water.

That's it, the Draugr spoke to her, gentle and reassuring as it held her head under the surface with its skeletal fingers, *just let go.*

Mera's necklace sent a bolt of pure power into her chest, filling her body with strength. She let the energy surge within her and, remembering her training with Ida, forced it outward, forming a protective shield all around her.

The shield collided with the Draugr. It flew backward and disappeared into the dark water.

Mera surfaced, air filling her lungs as she coughed and sputtered. The stench was stronger than ever, tainting the air that she so desperately needed. The current of energy flowed between her and her shield, steadying her in the water like a buoy.

Mera swam toward the shore, fighting her way back through the waves. She had only gone a few feet when the Draugr's raspy laughter filled her head once again.

Going somewhere? the Draugr chuckled.

Something moved by her right foot, and she kicked hard, trying to propel herself toward the beach.

What's waiting for you there, Mera?

She saw Ani waving from the shore, shouting something she couldn't hear.

Oh yes, your friends. The ones you have forced here, against their will?

It was Mera's fault they were here. They had tried to back out, and Mera had tricked them. Manipulated them. Used them.

Perhaps you are returning to your family?

Something swept by her leg. The effort of keeping her shield up was almost too much. Her necklace pulsed on her chest.

Yes, Mera, hurry home to your grandmother, the Draugr cooed, *as if the woman hasn't been through enough.*

A series of images flashed through Mera's mind: Ida standing over Darcy, her face covered in tears; Ida sitting in her grand dining room, eating dinner alone; Mera hitting Ida with a burst of energy and running out the front door.

You're not safe anywhere. Or should I say, nowhere is safe from you?

The Draugr's voice was seeping into her brain like poison, underneath the heavy fog that had invaded her mind a week ago. Mera had focused so much energy on keeping Ida out of her mind, she had left it open for the Draugr to sneak right in. The fog, the ringing, the intense anger, sadness, and isolation, the voice in her mind encouraging her to be her worst self—it was all this creature's doing.

The Draugr emerged in front of her, repelled by the shield but close enough to make Mera scream. It laughed, the sound piercing her mind like needles. Her necklace pulsed weaker still, threatening to give out. The smell of the rotting creature so intense now, Mera thought she might pass out.

But I don't have to tell you, do I, Mera? You're a real live-wire, as they say. A beacon, shining in the long dark night.

The Draugr contorted its face into an expression of soft admiration. Mera closed her eyes and tried to swim forward, willing her shield in front of her.

I saw you that day—peering over the cliff. Do you

remember?

Mera flashed back to her second day at Ida's. How she had looked into the water and saw the dark shape under the waves, its influence pulling at her.

I have only ever felt power like yours once. The chaos inside, the lack of control. I knew I had to have you. All I had to do was wait.

She opened her eyes. The Draugr was closer than ever now. Her necklace turned cold, its heartbeat stopped. It was all she could do to keep herself afloat.

You don't belong with them. Swim back to the beach, but we both know who will suffer if you do. . . .

Mera dipped below the surface of the water, her shield dying out as her eyes slipped shut. The Draugr was right. The danger she posed to the people she was fighting to get back to —she had known it all along. Her mother's face surfaced in her mind, and a pang of grief gripped her heart.

Ahh, we've gotten there at last, have we? the Draugr wheezed. *Have you not figured it out yet? What happened to Mommy?*

The Draugr let out a low laugh. It echoed in Mera's head.

A hand closed over her ankle. Unable to fight, she let it drag her under. Staring up at the surface, the darkness of the sea swallowed her. It was her fault her mother was gone.

Oh yes, you're something special. Why do you think she hid you for so long? asked the Draugr as it pulled her deeper into the water. *Moving you around, keeping you from anyone or anything that would recognize you for what you are. Giving up so much.*

Mera was sinking. Whatever was inside of her had driven

her mother away.

I know, the Draugr cooed, *but it will all be over soon. You're with me now, and you'll never have to worry about hurting anyone else ever again.*

The Draugr placed its rotted hand on her cheek, and Mera's remaining energy seeped into it. This is what the Draugr was after—her energy—but she didn't care. The Draugr could have it. It had never done her any good. Only caused her and the people around her pain. She just wanted it to end.

Mera's mother's face flashed in her mind.

Mera's necklace pulsed.

The water is yours, Mera, her mother's voice called to her. *Find yourself and fight.*

Her words rippled in Mera's mind. Mera focused on the water all around her—the way it enclosed her, how it flowed through her outstretched fingers and fanned out her hair. The water swirled around her, its energy flowing into her body and bubbled in her chest. Her necklace returned to life, its heartbeat cheering on Mera's own.

No, no no no, the Draugr whined. *This is not how this goes.*

Suspended now in the cold, silent darkness of the raging ocean, Mera understood what it meant to be an Undine.

Mera lifted her hand and sent a pulse of energy outward, hitting the Draugr and sending it backward.

Mera kicked to the surface, her vision going in and out. She gasped for breath. The storm raged on, tossing the waves harder than ever, but the water buoyed underneath her, its energy helping to keep her afloat.

Lightning struck again, and thunder rolled. Mera breathed in every crackle of energy in the air.

Mera swam as hard as she could toward the beach. Her necklace pulsed warmth into her body as she made her way closer. Her head was clear, the fog and anxiety gone for good. The stench evaporated. Whatever psychic hold the Draugr had over her was broken.

She was close enough to the shore that her feet touched sand, and she dragged herself through the water, searching the beach for her friends. Wyatt and Ani were nowhere in sight.

Mera sensed the Draugr behind her, but too late. It tackled her, and she fell forward, the impossible weight of the creature on her back. It pinned her in the shallow water, its hands on her head, ripping her energy from her now. Mera screamed, her voice gargling under the water as her head was split apart.

It could have been so peaceful, like going to sleep, the Draugr hissed. *But if you want the life torn from you, the Draugr can accommodate.*

Mera freed one of her hands and directed another pulse of energy at the Draugr, sending it flying back off her.

Mera pushed herself up, trying to stand. Her wet hair was in her eyes, clinging to her face, making it impossible to see. She pushed at it with one hand while casting out her senses, just as the Draugr launched itself at her again. She waved her hand, but her energy didn't connect with the creature. It had vanished.

Mera, Mera, Mera. This is not a fight you will win. All that power, but no idea how to use it. It will eat you alive before I even get the chance.

Mera closed her eyes and focused on the small pearl of energy in her chest. She let it build inside of her, rising and moving through her body, its power building to a crescendo inside her. Her necklace melted into her chest, becoming one with her, as the energy moved into every pore of her skin.

With every breath, Mera connected to more power, not just from the water at her feet, but from everywhere. The air she breathed in, the sand underneath her, the electric charge of the lightning crackling in the sky. And from another source that Mera couldn't pinpoint. It was cold and mingled with the heat of her own energy, extinguishing and steaming and expanding.

Everything around her went still, but inside, she ignited.

She sensed the Draugr materialize, drawn to her like a magnet now. She opened her eyes and saw it standing before her.

Beautiful, so beautiful, it whimpered.

The Draugr reached out its hand and took a step closer. It looked into Mera's eyes, and in the blackened sockets, she saw the awe, and then the fear.

So much destruction, and it begins with me.

Mera's energy burst out into the world like an exploding supernova. It tore straight through the Draugr, pulling apart each of its particles and scattering them on the wind into nothingness.

Mera sank to her knees, ankle deep in water. She was hot and cold at once, her body wracked with sweat and chills. No matter how much air she drew into her lungs, it wasn't enough, and she held out a hand to stop from falling face first into the surf.

Next to her hand fell the most delicate white crystal that dissolved as it hit the water. The thunderstorm stopped—no more lightning or rain. Instead, it was snowing.

Mera got to her feet and looked behind her. Ani and Wyatt were standing together, wearing twin expressions of shock. Ida strode across the sand from the steps in the cliff face, tears streaming down her cheeks.

Mera looked at her tingling hands. Darcy's wild eyes flashed in her mind, filled with cold, shimmering might. Mera understood now what it was to harness the power of pure essence—just like her great-aunt.

"I'm an Aether," she whispered, her tears freezing before turning to steam as they fell onto her icy, burning skin.

TWENTY-SIX

MERA WAS STILL staring at her hands when Ida's hand rested on her shoulder. She turned and looked into her grandmother's eyes. They held each other's gaze for a long moment. Ida took Mera's arm and guided her out of the water.

Ida put her arm around Mera, hugging her close as they walked. Mera stared down at the rocky sand as she passed Wyatt and Ani. They fell into step behind them. The snow continued to fall.

Ida led them back up the cliff steps, along the path and through the back door, leaving them shivering in the kitchen. Mera looked at the ground, her mind and body numb, dripping water onto the floor. Damp from the rain and shaking, Wyatt and Ani stood on either side of her.

Mera jumped when Wyatt's hand touched her shoulder. She didn't look at him but allowed him to rest it there. On her other side, Ani slipped her hand into Mera's. Mera almost pulled away, considering what she was and what it would mean. But she didn't. Just like during the ritual, their energies found each other, intermingling and binding.

Ida reentered the room a few moments later, brandishing

dry clothes, blankets, and a stern expression.

"Go change, all of you," she said as she handed out the dry garments.

"We—" Ani began, but Ida held up her hand.

"Once you are dry and warm, we'll speak about what happened. And about what's next," Ida said before sweeping them from the kitchen.

***

After Mera had showered and changed, Ida ushered her into one of the drawing rooms, instructing her to wait there for the others, then left again to prepare tea.

As Mera took a seat in one of the tufted couches, a small gasp escaped her. Every part of her ached. Her throat was raw, and her eyes burned from the salt water.

It returned in a rush—the scene at the Convergence, discovering that Ida hadn't killed Darcy, the fight with the Draugr, and realizing what she was.

An Aether. Mera's heart fluttered, beating against her ribcage like a trapped bird. She gripped the side of the couch and took ragged breaths.

The door opened, and Ida stepped inside, carrying a tray. Ida set the tray down in front of Mera and sat beside her. She lifted a glass of water.

"Drink," Ida instructed, her voice stern but gentle.

Mera took the cup from her, sipping the water. It was blissful on her raw throat, and she closed her eyes from the relief. She tipped the glass, gulping now.

"Slowly, Mera," Ida said, reaching out to steady the glass.

Mera finished the water, and Ida turned back to the tray. There was toast alongside a steaming cup of tea. Ida picked up the cup and saucer.

"This now," she said, holding it out to Mera.

Mera set down the empty glass and accepted the tea. She was glad to have Ida there, telling her what to do. It saved her from having to do any thinking herself.

"Ida—"

"No," Ida stopped her.

"But—"

"We have a long and difficult conversation ahead of us. Eat and drink. I'm going to get the others."

The grandfather clock in the corner chimed with the start of a new hour. Mera almost choked on her tea when she saw what time it was—5:00 a.m. How was that possible? It was around 10:30 p.m. when they started the ritual.

When Ida returned, she had Wyatt and Ani in tow, each dressed in ill-fitting clothes. Instant relief filled Mera at the sight of them.

They sat next to Mera on the couch. Ida gave them each water, tea, and toast, instructing them through each as she had done for Mera.

Sitting together in silence, only broken by the clinking of a glass or the soft crunch of the bread, Mera studied Wyatt and Ani, but they appeared unhurt. Whatever the Draugr had done to them had left no physical mark.

"So," Ani broke the silence, cradling her tea. "Mera's an Aether."

Mera's eyes darted to Ida, who answered with a heavy sigh. "She is."

"How long have you known?" Wyatt asked.

"Since the moment she arrived."

"Why didn't you tell me?" Mera stared at Ida, who looked back at her.

"When we first spoke about Aethers, Mera, I felt your fear. If you were afraid of what you are, you would never trust yourself. I hoped that if you could learn control first, dealing with the rest would be . . . easier."

A long pause passed between them. If she learned she was an Aether during that first conversation with Ida about being an Elemental, it would have been overwhelming. Even now, the reality of it tugged at her seams, threatening to pull her apart.

"What am I?" Mera whispered.

"Well," Ida began, her voice firm. "Foremost, you are my granddaughter and an Undine. Second, you are an Aether.

"Aethers are rare and are only Undine women. Aethers have access to a different energy source, beyond their own Element. What that source of energy is—there are stories that the Aether was the first Element and is what the other Elements were born from. It's what makes Aethers so powerful. And what makes them so dangerous, in the eyes of many."

"Do you think I'm dangerous?"

"I do not," Ida assured her. "But if others find out, they will."

"I don't think you're dangerous," Wyatt said, his voice above a whisper. "I know you aren't."

Ani nodded in agreement, her wide eyes staring right into Mera's.

"That's all well and good," Ida said. "But I meant people outside of this house."

"We won't tell anyone," Ani promised, reaching over and taking Mera's hand. But Mera saw the worry on Ida's face.

"Ida, what is it?"

"An Aether's full power being released was sure to be felt around the village. Wyatt and Ani, we need to get you home," Ida said, peering out the window into the early morning darkness.

A chill went through Mera at the idea of being separated from Wyatt and Ani. They scooted closer to Mera.

"In a bit, then," Ida sighed, resigned.

"How did you know to come down to the beach?" Mera asked.

"I ran to the house to get her—the Draugr blocked me from teleporting," Ani said.

"I should have known when I couldn't sense your nightmares it was the influence of a Draugr. It's been so long since I've had to worry about things like that."

The Draugr's words came back to Mera. *Hadn't Ida been through enough?*

"I cannot express to you how dangerous it was to be on the beach at all, never mind performing that ritual. Do you know what you've done?"

"We looked into the past. It worked. I mean, we're all okay," Ani insisted.

"There are consequences to that ritual beyond it going wrong. You joined your energies. That can never be undone. You are bound together now. Forever," Ida stared between the three of them.

"But . . . that's a good thing, right?" Wyatt thought aloud.

Mera, Wyatt, and Ani looked at each other. The warmth in

Mera's core where their connection lived flickered.

"Let's hope so," Ida's voice cut in. "Why would you attempt something so dangerous in the first place?"

"I thought it might help—that there might be some clue about my mom. But . . ."

"Instead, you saw that I did not kill my sister."

Wyatt and Ani gasped.

"I'm the only one who saw. Wyatt and Ani got pulled back into the present before that, but I stayed behind somehow."

"Well, that's another thing I'll ask you not to share outside of this room," Ida said, looking between Wyatt and Ani.

"What did you do to Darcy?" Mera asked.

"I had every intention of killing her, but when it came down to it . . . she was . . ."

"She was your sister," Wyatt completed her thought.

"With all that she had done, she was cut off from the source of her power already. She severed her connection to her family, her community, her Element. Herself. She could only use energy she took from those around her. Our fight depleted all her stolen energy. I was patient. I let her use it all up. Then I bound her, so she'd never be able to access her power again."

"But—if Aethers are these all-powerful energy vacuums, how could Darcy ever be cut off?" Ani asked.

"Aethers are still Elementals. They exist within the same laws of our nature. If more people understood that, perhaps the fear of them would lessen," Ida said.

Mera found relief in the idea something still anchored an Aether.

"If Darcy isn't dead . . . where is she?" Ani shuddered.

"There's an Elemental village by the Great Lakes. They had an Aether generations ago that needed to be—contained. They built a special facility, the only one of its kind."

"An Aether prison," Mera murmured to herself.

"Not a prison in purpose. When Darcy started to lose control, I contacted them. If we could get her there, offer her structure and safety, maybe she would return to herself."

Ida broke off and looked away, the ghost of her failed plan to save her sister written all over her pained face.

"They did not arrive in time," Ida continued. "It was too late to save her, the Darcy I knew. They agreed to take what was left of her, put her in the facility."

"And she's still there?" Wyatt whispered.

Ida shook her head. "She died a few years later. I was told she withered away to nothing."

"She was a monster, Ida. You did what you had to do," Mera said.

"The person you saw at the Convergence was not my sister. Being born an Aether marked her in our family and our community. In the entire Elemental world. People feared her, monitored her. Our own parents—" Ida's voice became hard. "Her power defined her in the eyes of others, and so it came to define her in her own mind. I was the only one who saw her for who she was. For Darcy.

"As she grew, so did her powers, and so did the fear of her. People blamed her for anything that went wrong in the village. She tried to blend in, then she tried to isolate herself, but it was never enough. She told me if they were going to hate her either way, she would rather be hated for being her truest, most powerful self. That's when she began to abuse her gifts."

Mera remembered what Rochester said about the disoriented Terra boy—how that used to happen more often.

"By the time I realized what was happening, it was too late to stop her. Darcy became so entangled in her powers. She couldn't separate herself from them anymore. She didn't want to."

Mera flashed back to the beach—how she consumed the surrounding energy like a black hole before unleashing it back out of herself. A shiver ran through her, and goosebumps erupted on her arms. It had felt . . . good.

"When the council discovered what Darcy was doing, they voted to Quell her."

Ani gasped, and Wyatt's face drained of color at the word.

"Quell her?" Mera asked.

"The Terras have practiced it for thousands of years. A Quelling is the ultimate punishment for an Elemental, even worse than death. It's a ritual that neutralizes the energy of an Elemental so severely, it severs the connection to their energy —to their essence. It leaves you alive but unfeeling, unthinking. A Quelling is the cruelest and most barbaric tradition that exists in our world."

"But why couldn't they bind and imprison her, like you were planning?" Wyatt asked.

"It was too late for mercy, they believed. Our own mother was the head of the council, and she led the vote to Quell Darcy. That's what untethered Darcy entirely. She vowed to take their powers before they could take hers.

"She started with our mother and our father. The rest of our family came next, and then the council. And anyone who tried to stop her—including my husband."

Mera felt stupid. She had never considered Ida being married before, or even who her grandfather was. Now she realized he was another victim of Darcy.

"She only spared your mother and me," Ida continued. "She believed I was on her side, the only one who understood what she was doing. And she loved your mother like her own daughter. It was the only real piece of her that remained."

Ani reached out and took Ida's hand. Ida was taken aback at first but accepted her comfort.

"I almost didn't fight her. But when I realized there was no one else to stop her, I knew I didn't have a choice."

They sat in silence for a long time.

"It is vital that no one ever discovers you are an Aether, Mera. Darcy's legacy is too strong in the history of our community. People lost their families that day. If they were to find out you were an Aether, they would not see reason. Everyone outside of this room is a threat to you. To us." Ida turned to look at Mera, her eyes shining.

Mera nodded. Another beat of silence passed between them. Mera understood what Ida was saying but couldn't help thinking she was more of a threat to others than they were to her. She put Wyatt and Ani in danger to get answers about her mom—answers she didn't even find.

"Mera, what is it?" Ida asked, peering into her granddaughter's face.

"Darcy said something about my mom. Something about what would happen to her."

Ida sighed. "Darcy put little faith in the Old Ways. She believed the laws our mother and the other Elementals in power enforced were meant to stifle and oppress us. She wanted to free your mother from that, to let her grow up without boundaries. Our systems aren't perfect, but Darcy called for the destruction of our history and our most ancient bonds."

Mera understood why Ida would find this rejection of tradition so troubling, as someone who so staunchly subscribed to the Old Ways. But the Terras in power didn't share Ida's utopian ethos. Rochester and his allies had twisted the Old Ways to intimidate, to isolate, to oppress. Maybe Darcy had been right.

"There's something else. . . ." Mera pushed forward, remembering how her mother had appeared to her in the Convergence to warn her about the Draugr.

But Ida's eyes widened. The wave of recognition hit them both at the same time.

The Terra police were racing up the driveway, heading straight for the house.

TWENTY-SEVEN

IDA SWEPT INTO action as headlights crested over the hill. Mera, Wyatt, and Ani trailed behind her. Ida halted at the front door and cast out her senses.

"They're here for a diamond," Ida said, turning back to Mera, Wyatt, and Ani. "What diamond?"

"It's on the beach," Ani gasped, her hand flying over her mouth.

Mera saw two figures run past the front porch, heading for the beach.

"I'll teleport to it, get it before they can," Ani said in a rush, but Ida grabbed her arm.

"You'll do no such thing. You will take Wyatt and Mera to your grandfather. Tell him what's happening," Ida instructed, steering Ani, Wyatt, and Mera away from the front door.

"No, what about you?" Mera demanded.

"I'll be fine, Mera, but you must go."

Ani took Mera's hand, and the air swirled. Ida turned to the front door, ready to take on whatever came through.

At the last moment, Mera withdrew her hand from Ani's. Wyatt's eyes widened with alarm as he disappeared into the wind along with Ani.

"I won't leave you," Mera insisted.

Ida whirled around, intense annoyance straining her features. Before Ida could respond, the front door crashed down, and police streamed into the house. Ida pushed Mera behind her.

Say nothing, Ida commanded in her mind. *Do not use your powers.*

Rochester pushed through the throng of officers, his expression smug and hungry.

"Search the house," Rochester demanded. The officers began tearing the place apart, turning out drawers and smashing items. Some raced upstairs to do the same on other floors.

Mera's necklace turned fiery hot and twitched as Rochester got closer, her snarling guard dog. Ida's resentment blanketed the surrounding air.

"I see you are conducting warrantless raids on private property now, Rochester," Ida said. "A real high point of your legacy, I'm sure."

"Grab them," Rochester barked, gesturing to his men.

Before Mera could even think, Ida's shield cut through the air with a thwap, sending the two officers closest to them stumbling backward.

"One old woman against twenty trained Terras?" Rochester barked, laughing. "Be reasonable for once, Ida."

"Get out of my house."

Rochester laughed again.

"Break down her shield."

I can help you! Mera pleaded in Ida's mind as the Terras

jostled into striking position.

No, Ida replied, a note of panic in her voice. *You are not to use your powers under any circumstances.*

A shout came from the porch as the two Terras returned from the beach. They shouldered their way to Rochester, one of them placing something heavy in his hand. His eyes glazed over with a maniacal joy. It was the diamond.

"Did you know that one of my girls has a very special gift? I've never seen anything like it before, amazing. She can sense powerful rocks and crystals, other Terra objects—she can speak to them, in a way."

Rochester moved closer to them, and the officers fell into defensive formation behind him. "So, you can imagine my surprise when she sensed this diamond—my diamond—was not where it should be. The diamond told her something awful was done to it—a force altered its energy. It told her that if we went to your beach, we would find it. And now I'm left wondering what power can corrupt an object as strong and ancient as this diamond?"

Ida sent an image to Mera's mind: Mera on the beach sending the shockwave of Aether energy toward the Draugr. The shockwave splintered in every direction, dissipating before reaching Ida but connecting with the diamond.

"What did you do to it?" Rochester asked through gritted teeth.

Ida considered him and then said, "That is none of your concern."

Rochester's eyes blazed. "So you admit it! You admit to stealing a powerful Terra artifact and tampering with it."

Ida, no! Mera tried to scream at Ida, but Ida had blocked

her from her mind.

"Yes," Ida said.

Rochester looked around, making sure everyone else was hearing the same thing.

"Ida Kellen, you are under arrest. Lower your shield and come quietly, or we will take you by force," Rochester ordered, relishing the moment.

"I will lower my shield on the condition that Mera is unharmed. She had no part in this; I acted alone."

Rochester's eyes jumped back and forth between them.

"Fine, as long as neither of you gives us any more trouble."

"Give me your word."

Rochester sighed like an impatient child. "You have my word. Now lower your shield."

With an exhale, Ida's shield vanished. The Terra energy that had been up against it flooded into Ida. Ida's body constricted, and her knees gave out. She tried to hide the pain in her expression, but she couldn't.

"Stop it! What are you doing to her!" Mera yelled.

Rochester turned to Mera. "Is that trouble I hear?"

He held out his hand toward her, and a heaviness entered Mera's body that was too strong for her necklace to fend off. Her own energy was being used against her, forced to sink down within her like a stone. Buried. She sank to the ground next to Ida.

"Your word means nothing," Ida spat, her face contorted in pain.

"My officers here could see how hostile she was. I was afraid for their safety!" He shrugged, standing over them. "We know that your kind is dangerous. We've seen the destruction this family has caused."

Rochester tightened his grip on her energy as he spoke. Mera's eyes watered. She strained to breathe. Through her bleary eyes, she saw Rochester step toward her. He reached out and wrapped his hand around her necklace, which zapped him feebly. He laughed, then ripped it off her neck and put it in his pocket. Mera's tears spilled over.

"I've been telling this village for years about the threat that you posed. And now, they will see I was right. They will see how those who threaten us are punished."

He looked at his men, his eyes gleaming with a crazed anticipation. "Take them to the Convergence. Round up everyone. Drag them out of their beds if you have to. I want them all to see this."

Hands encircled her arms and lifted her. They took her outside and dumped her into the back of a police car with Ida. Rochester got into the front seat. He turned around to look at them, constricted under his power.

"What a proud day for the Kellens," he smiled at them.

He started the car and led the caravan back down the driveway.

Mera, Ida's voice was back in her mind, *don't be afraid.*

What is going on? Mera thought back.

Before Ida could answer, pain seared behind her eyes, as though someone had just gripped her brain.

"None of that telepathy crap," Rochester barked from the front seat. "No more of it ever."

Beside her, Ida took a deep breath and closed her eyes. She appeared to be in deep concentration. Mera's mind was in chaos, but she tried to remember what Ida had said about controlling herself. She closed her eyes and tried to ignore the constricting pain and calm herself as the car lurched forward.

By the time they arrived at the Convergence, Mera thought she might black out. She was barely aware of the car stopping, the door opening, and being dragged out. Mera blinked and recognized they were moving up a small hill at one end of the Convergence, the side opposite the cliff.

Early morning light was breaking over the horizon, giving the field a cold, purple glow. There was a thin coat of snow on the ground.

The more they jostled Mera around as they made their way up the hill, the more she could feel the shape of Rochester's power inside her body. Her own energy began coursing around the binding force, probing for a weak point. Mera had not forgotten Ida's warning to avoid using her powers at all costs, but it continued to scale and coil around the invading energy. She wasn't sure how long she could keep it at bay.

The officers deposited Mera and Ida on the hill, so they were visible to the crowds of people assembling below. The villagers gasped when they caught sight of Ida and her. The Terra police were yelling, directing the crowds forward.

"Here she is, here she is," Rochester called out, pointing to Ida.

Tara reached the front of the assembled crowd, clad in pajamas and holding the hands of two small, identical twin girls. Mera could only assume they were her sisters. Tara's puzzled glance flitted back and forth from Ida and Mera to her father, who took one of the young girls up into his arms.

"You made this happen, my special gem," Rochester gushed at the girl in his arms. She beamed back at him.

"What's going on?" Tara asked, her voice shaking. The sister still clutching her hand hid behind Tara's legs in fear.

"This is it, my little flower. This is the day we've been waiting for," Rochester said, placing his free hand around Tara's shoulders, his voice filled with tender pride. "I wanted you girls to be right here with me. It's history."

Rochester steered his daughters into place just behind him, placing the twin in his arms back down. Tara took her hand once again as she tried to comfort her other sister by stroking her hair.

Rochester strode out in front of Ida and Mera, facing the crowd of Elementals. The field had filled up with villagers. He turned to smirk at Ida and Mera. Mera's energy flared, crashing against her insides like an angry wave against a pane of glass. Rochester's smile faltered for the briefest moment, and then he closed his open hand into a fist, doubling his vice-like grip. Her mouth fell open, and with a small gasp, she toppled forward onto the grass. A few people cried out in the crowd.

Hands gripped her shoulders and forced her back to a sitting position.

Rochester cleared his throat, and a hush fell over the crowd. Whether it was out of respect, fear, or curiosity, it was hard to tell.

"I have gathered you here today to bear witness to this historic moment. Today, we will eradicate the gravest threat to our community's safety. A threat that has held our village hostage for decades—the Kellen family."

The crowd broke into murmurs, but Rochester continued.

"Since the day their bloodline produced the Aether, they

have cursed our village! I have known, since the day that murderer struck down my father in cold blood, along with so many of your fathers, and families, that the Kellen bloodline is a tainted lineage. Evil incarnate."

Rochester held up the diamond.

"Today, Ida Kellen confessed to not only the theft of this powerful Terra artifact, but to attempting to tamper with its energy for her own nefarious purposes," he spat. "Who knows what kind of destruction she would have rained down if she succeeded. But, as we all know, Terra energy bows to no other Element."

He turned and faced Ida, a smug victory on his face as the Terra police broke into applause. Mera glanced over at Tara, who was staring at the diamond, frozen.

"I also discovered, to no one's surprise," Rochester continued, turning back to his audience, "that her granddaughter, Mera Kellen, aided in the act."

Mera's anger boiled white hot within her again. Rochester's grip on her loosened ever-so-slightly against the heat.

"For these reasons, I put them before you, as an example of what happens to those who threaten our community," Rochester boomed, righteous fury rising in his voice. "To those who believe they are above our laws and oppose our traditions and values. Today will go down in history as the day I rid Convergence of evil, once and for all!"

Rochester's fists clenched at his sides, shaking. Ida looked out into the crowd, laser-focused on a point in the distance.

"Today, with the village as witness, Ida and Mera Kellen will be Quelled."

Mera's heart dropped. With a surge of frenetic energy, cries of disapproval sounded in the crowd. There was a shout from somewhere near the back. Was that Wyatt's voice? Mera saw Tara shift beside them, taking a step away from Ida, Mera, and her father.

Rochester's voice boomed over them all. "Today, we will have the punishment owed to us for Darcy Kellen. Today, we will have the justice we deserved all those years ago!"

The Terra police cheered, but louder now were the villagers crying out in protest.

"From now on," Rochester continued to shout over the rising volume of the crowd, "I will meet any threat to our way of life with swift, merciless punishment!"

Rochester turned and nodded to the Terra officers behind Mera and Ida. There were nine or ten of them, Mera couldn't tell, and they stepped forward to surround them. Mera's energy seared through her, and Mera shook, feeling like it was about to shoot out through her skin.

A deep male voice boomed over the crowd of villagers.

"The winds have changed. The time has come."

Everyone turned to the center of the crowd—an old man with bright white hair floated above them.

"Vihaan!" Rochester roared, looked to the Terra police assembled before him, who mirrored his confusion. "Take— take him!" he screamed.

The man in the air disappeared, and then everything was chaos.

TWENTY-EIGHT

THE TERRA POLICE who still flanked Ida and Mera blocked Mera's vision. But she felt the fight erupt in the clearing below, alive with the energy of the Elementals. Sylphs, Salamanders, Terras—their energy was electric and intoxicating.

Rochester cried out, "*Begin!*"

The Terra police surrounding Ida and Mera jostled each other, hesitating.

"I said *begin!*" Rochester screeched.

One of the Terra officers steeled himself and faced them, and a few others followed his lead. They raised their hands.

The air lightened around them, and one of the Terra officers disappeared.

The other officers spun around, searching for the unseen enemy. Another Terra disappeared, then another. One of them ran but was plucked away in the thinning atmosphere. Mera realized it must be an invisible Sylph, teleporting the Terra police away, one by one.

An eruption of heat next to her prickled Mera's skin, and she turned to see Ida was now free of the Terra's grip. Ida's surge of power entered Mera's chest and swelled inside her to break Rochester's constraints. Air rushed into her body again, and her eyes watered with relief.

The remaining Terra police backed away from Ida as she got to her feet. Ida stretched out her hand and knocked them back even further.

Mera sensed Rochester behind them, getting ready to attack. She whipped around to face him.

"No!" Mera yelled as she unleashed a wave of furious energy with her hand.

Rochester's eyes widened as the energy collided with him and sent him flying. He landed hard on the ground.

"Dad!" Tara shouted, running to his side.

Mera thought of her necklace and took a step toward Rochester. Tara scrambled to her feet and moved in front of her father, her hands clenching at her sides. Her eyes flitted to her sisters, crouched a few feet away.

Mera felt a familiar lightness cut through the air between them. The air shimmered, and Ani materialized, standing beside Tara. She took Tara by the arm.

"No, don't! Dad, help!" Tara yelled, turning back to her dad, who had taken the momentary distraction as a chance to escape. Tara watched her father run without even looking back at her before she vanished back into the air along with Ani. A moment later, Mera saw her sisters disappear, too.

Beside Mera, Ida fell to one knee. She had been taking on the Terra officers alone, but after Ida used her reserve of energy to break them free of the Terra's grip, they were starting to overpower her.

Without thinking, Mera reached out and grabbed Ida's

hand. She let her own energy flow into Ida, replenishing her strength. Ida looked at her in shock before Mera pulled her to her feet. Working as one, they emitted a shockwave that collided with the Terras. They hit the ground hard, and none of them tried to stand again.

Mera turned back, scanning the clearing, but Rochester was gone. And so was her necklace.

She looked in front of her at the crowd below. The Terra police dropped to their knees, surrendering. To Mera's surprise, other Terras were helping the Sylphs and Salamanders subdue and restrain them.

A figure materialized in front of them. It was the Sylph who had called the village to action. He had the severe expression of an aged history professor.

"This was not the way we meant it to happen, Ida," the man spoke. His voice was familiar to Mera, but she couldn't place it.

"I understand that, Vihaan, but circumstances were beyond my control," Ida responded, gesturing all around her.

"Fighting among members of the community will have a severe ripple effect. I can sense it in the air already. Our energy shield is at the weakest it's ever been now," Vihaan pressed.

"The barrier's protection wasn't going to hold for much longer. Now, with Rochester out of power, we can mend it," Ida reassured him. "It wasn't what we planned, but it'll work out the same way."

A scene floated into her mind of Vihaan and Ida in her study late at night, surrounded by swirling hot air. It all clicked.

"Wait, so you've been planning this all along? Overthrowing Rochester?" Mera asked, astonished. "I heard you in our house, in Ida's study!"

Vihaan smiled at her and nodded. He held out his hand. "Vihaan Joshi."

"Ani's grandfather?" Mera questioned, shaking his hand.

Others joined them on the hill. Mera sensed Salamanders, more Sylphs, and several Terras.

"I've heard a lot about you, Mera," Vihaan continued.

Mera jumped as Ani materialized next to her and put her hand on Mera's shoulder.

"Only good stuff! Selective stuff," Ani whispered to Mera. Vihaan rolled his eyes.

Wyatt and his parents made their way over, as well. Mera's heart flipped at the sight of him. His pace quickened until he was half jogging to her, then he wrapped her in a hug.

"I'm so glad you're all right," Wyatt breathed in her ear. Mera returned the hug, welcoming his soothing warmth.

"Has anyone seen Rochester?" Mrs. Hall's voice broke into their embrace. Mera and Wyatt pulled apart.

Mera blushed and glanced at Ani, who stifled a grin. She turned to see Ida staring between her and Wyatt with a grave expression.

"No one can account for him," Vihaan answered.

"He's gone," Mera said, trying to push through her embarrassment. "He ran toward the woods."

Vihaan nodded. "We need an emergency meeting of the council while a search party looks for Rochester. We'll have to detain the remaining Terra police until the council has decided what to do with them."

"You three," Ida turned to Mera, Ani, and Wyatt. "We have much to do. Until then, do try not to incite any more civil wars, will you?"

The adults got to work assigning roles. Mera, Ani, and Wyatt sat down on the hill. Mera felt her body relax for the first time since Rochester had shown up at Ida's door. She inched closer to her friends, seeking their comforting energies.

"Okay," Ani said with a tone of resignation. "You're mad, just say it."

"What?" Wyatt asked.

"You're totally mad at me. I don't even have to read minds to tell. I stole the diamond, this is all my fault, I never should have taken it, honestly, I was just caught up in the thrill of stealing from nasty old Rochester and doing the ritual, you know? I even wore black and everything, even though I was like, invisible—"

"Ani!" Mera broke into Ani's rambling apology. "It's okay! We wouldn't have done that ritual if it weren't for me."

"Ani, maybe you should take credit for it. That diamond kind of started a revolution," Wyatt shrugged.

Ani's eyes went wide. "Revolution," she whispered to herself.

"The Terras have been in power forever. What's going to happen now?" Wyatt wondered.

"I guess that's what the council is going to decide," Mera nodded toward the group of concerned adults. They were huddled together, speaking in hushed voices. Mera saw Patrick join the group, the Terra officer who had come to Ida's about Clay. Was he part of this so-called resistance?

A woman appeared out of nowhere behind Vihaan. She looked alarmed.

"Vihaan, Ida, we need you," she said, her voice full of fear.

Vihaan spun to face her. "Is it Rochester?"

"No. It's—someone else."

"Who?" Ida demanded.

"She was in the woods. We found her inside our border, but she's out of her head, covered in dirt. She said she was looking for her daughter," the woman responded, her eyes darting to Mera.

Mera's heart clenched.

"Where is she?" Mera said, pushing herself up and jogging toward the group.

"Down there," the woman replied, nodding to the bottom of the hill.

"Mera, wait!" Ida's voice called out to her.

But Mera didn't stop. She ran as fast as she could down the hill. The search party members started at her sudden arrival, but Mera focused on the woman they were holding between them.

Her mother.

"Mom?" Mera whispered, her small voice lost in the wind.

Genevieve was filthy. Her hair was long and tangled, darkened from being unwashed. She was scratched and bruised, covered in dirt and mud. She was shaking, her eyes fixed on the ground in front of her. Mera knew beyond a doubt that this was her mother but seeing her this way—she was unrecognizable.

Wyatt arrived next to Mera, and he let out a small gasp. Mera sensed Ani a few steps behind them.

"What happened to her?" Ani breathed over her shoulder.

Mera reached out with her senses, but her mother's mind was blocked. She couldn't get a read on her at all.

Mera stepped forward, but the members of the search party put their hands out to stop her.

"She could be dangerous," one of them warned.

"That's my mother."

Mera took another step closer.

"Mom?" Mera said louder this time. "Mom, it's me."

But her mother's eyes were fixed on the ground. She mumbled something in a whispered tone.

"What?" Mera asked, leaning in closer.

"She said she needs to find her daughter. That's all she's been saying," one of the search party members said.

Mera stepped closer. "It's me, Mom. You found me. I'm here."

The council members descended the hill with Ida leading the pack.

"Ida, it's really her," Mera called out.

Ida moved forward, her expression grave. Mera's mother raised her head. She stared at Ida, her body stiffening. She brought her hands down to her sides, and her shaking stopped.

"You," Genevieve said, her voice contorted by anger.

Ida returned Genevieve's stare but said nothing. Mera moved closer to her mom, trying to put herself in her line of vision. But Genevieve would only look at Ida. Mera put her hands on her mother's arms. They were ice cold.

"Mom, what's going on?" she asked, desperate.

"Mera, step away from her," Ida called, an edge to her

voice.

Mera turned to look at Ida. "What? No. She needs help."

Ida took another step closer to them. Mera could see her expression better now. She had gone white.

"That is not Genevieve," Ida breathed.

Mera looked at her mother as Genevieve's features pulled into a lopsided smile.

"*Move!*" Ida cried as Mera's mother unleashed a wild wave of power at Ida. Mera was thrown aside, pushed out of the way by Ida's energy.

Mera hit the ground hard and rolled onto her back. Ida was crumpled on the ground, holding her chest. Instead of defending herself, she had saved Mera and taken her mother's full blast.

Genevieve took on everyone at once—the members of the search party and the council. More ran over to join the fight. Genevieve was screaming, as though with each discharge of energy she sent out, she was enduring incredible pain.

"No!" Mera cried out.

Her mother hit Patrick and sent him flying. She took out another, then another, her strength unmatched by any of them. Mera couldn't let this continue. She pushed herself to her feet and summoned all her power into her mind.

"*Mom, stop!*" Mera demanded. Her will slammed into Genevieve's mind with such force, it knocked her mother backward and off her feet.

When Mera reached her mother, she was blinking awake. Genevieve pushed herself into a sitting position as Mera kneeled at her side.

"Mom?" Mera asked.

"Mera?" her mom murmured.

Mera let out a strangled cry and grabbed her mother, pulling her into a hug. But her mom wrenched away.

"She's coming," she cried. "I can't hold her off. Please, go."

She pushed Mera away.

"Mom, wait, stop! I'm not leaving you!"

"Run, Mera! Please!"

Her face went blank again, her arms dropped to her sides like a limp doll.

An icy blast struck Mera on one side of her body that pierced her like razor-edged icicles. She slammed into the ground, the air leaving her lungs. Her vision blurred, and her skin burned and stung. There was an awful laughter then screams rang out from the villagers. Her vision cleared, and she could see people fleeing, their eyes wide with terror. Mera pushed herself up onto her elbows to take in what they saw.

A woman in a long, lace dress with pale, wild hair stood next to Genevieve. Her skin was glowing an icy blue.

Ida took a sharp intake of breath.

"Darcy."

TWENTY-NINE

"HELLO, SISTER." DARCY'S voice was low and melodic. She looked at Mera and grinned. "Hello, lovey."

Mera looked on from the ground, too shocked to stand. Darcy stroked Genevieve's hair. Her mother's blank eyes looked into Darcy's.

Mera turned to see Ida pull herself up, staring at Darcy in disbelief. Behind Ida, Mera saw members of the search party and council slinking toward the woods. The remaining Sylphs teleported as many away as they could.

Mr. Hall was leading Wyatt and Ani away by the arms toward the tree line. Ani couldn't take her eyes off Darcy, tears spilling down her cheeks. Wyatt was protesting, but when he locked eyes with Mera, she mouthed, "*Go!*"

The only members of the resistance who remained were Ida, Vihaan, Patrick, and Mrs. Hall.

Darcy's full attention was on Ida, her eyes boring into her sister.

"They told me you were dead," Ida said.

"They did, didn't they?" Darcy mused. "They were as weak as the prison they threw me in. It couldn't hold me, and neither could they."

Vihaan stepped closer to Ida, his confusion outweighing his fear. "I thought you killed her in the battle?"

Darcy laughed, overjoyed. "Is that what you told them? Oh, that's wonderful. Well done, Ida. Although, let's be honest. Small minds aren't difficult to fill with even smaller ideas, now are they? Ida did not kill me that day. She did something far worse."

When Darcy next spoke, a cool fury filled her voice.

"She bound me then had me thrown in a windowless cell. I didn't see the sun for years. . . ." Darcy trailed off, her eyes glinting. She rolled her head back and basked in the light of the rising sun. The early morning rays emphasized her cold glow. "But look at me now."

"Impossible," Ida whispered. "No Elemental can break a binding."

"No Elemental," Darcy regarded Ida again, her head cocked to the side. "But I am no mere Elemental. I was reborn. Of pure essence. It was beautiful."

Ida cast her senses out toward Darcy.

"You are not connecting to the energy around you anymore," Ida said, horror in her voice. "You are— consuming it, feeding off of it the same way a creature does."

Darcy laughed again, the joy returning. "I tapped into something else! The most ancient truth there ever was—The Aether."

Mera looked again at her mother, who was shaking and hugging herself.

Mera pulled herself to her feet. "Let my mother go."

Darcy's head snapped toward her, her face alive with

curiosity.

"Mera," Ida warned.

"Oh yes, my darling Mera. We haven't had the chance to meet yet. At least, not corporeally."

"Let. Her. Go," Mera commanded.

Darcy studied Mera, a smile creeping up the side of her lips. "Like looking in a mirror."

Mera sensed Ida move to release a bolt of energy at Darcy. At the same time, Vihaan disappeared into the wind, while Patrick held out his hands to neutralize Darcy's energy, and Mrs. Hall held up hers to put a protective shield around the five of them.

But Darcy sensed it, as Mera had. She beckoned to Mera with her finger, and the world fell away. Mera now stood alone with Darcy in the Convergence. Except it was night, the only light coming from the full moon.

"I take it that Ida hasn't explained the astral world to you yet?" Darcy chuckled. "Doesn't surprise me. She always feared anything that reminded her of how powerful we could be. Nothing's changed!

"What to say about the astral plane? It's a destination accessible only to a gifted few. And there's no one as gifted as us, Mera. This gives us a moment to chat. Alone."

A chill ran through Mera that had nothing to do with the weather in this impenetrable other dimension in which her murderous great-aunt had trapped her.

"What do you want with my mother?" Mera asked through gritted teeth, trying not to betray her rising sense of panic.

The world around them shifted again, so they were standing in a nursery. In the middle of the room was a crib that Darcy approached. She lifted out a baby.

"Genevieve was always darling to me. She never cried when I held her, you know. She was never afraid of me. Smiled every time she saw me."

The baby reached its small hand up to Darcy, chortling as it did.

"It was a pleasant change to have someone not flinch away from me. To have someone that loved me and accepted me, as I was."

The baby vanished as the nursery melted back into the Astral Convergence. Mera was dizzy from her reality changing at Darcy's whim.

"But they took me from her. Locked in that prison for years. As soon as I was free, I came for her. I couldn't get in, of course, with that pesky border. But then I discovered Genevieve had run off! I had hoped she realized the truth about Ida, and run away, maybe to search for me. I didn't know, of course, Ida lied about my fate. But if she couldn't find me, I would find her."

Darcy peered into Mera's face. Mera backed away.

"Genevieve was smart—staying in cities to dull her Elemental energy. But one beautiful day, I found, when I was still, I could sense this slow pulse of energy. It drew me to it. I wasn't sure what it was, but I had hoped it was your mother, reaching out to me," Darcy continued, circling around Mera now.

"And so, I went toward it but could never reach it. It grew stronger as time went on, until it was a second heartbeat," Darcy held a hand over her chest, simulating the feeling. "Then, one night—"

The world shifted again, and they were now standing on a lit street. Mera saw her mother walking toward her, her long dark hair flowing out behind her, her expression set and determined.

"I dreamed of that moment for a long time. But it did not go as I expected." Darcy looked up at Mera again, her eyes shimmering. Mera turned to see her mother raise her hands and send a blast of power straight at them. "I subdued her, of course. But I didn't understand why she would attack me this way until I realized . . . she wasn't the source of the heartbeat."

Everything changed again. Mera watched her mother and the street dissolve to darkness. In the dark, Mera could see a light glowing just ahead of them. She felt Darcy move toward that light as it pulsed, drumming like a beating heart.

"If it wasn't Genevieve calling out to me, then what was it? But she wouldn't tell me." Darcy's face was lit only by the glowing ball of light in front of her, making her skin appear more hallowed than ever. "So, when Genevieve would not cooperate—"

"You made her," Mera interrupted.

Revelations filled Mera's mind: their constant moving, the refusal to be near the water, the cement cityscapes that dotted their past, her mother's panic attacks and nightmares. Genevieve sensed an approaching threat and tried to keep Mera from whatever was coming. But once it found them, she went to meet the threat herself. Her mother couldn't have been expecting Darcy—everyone believed Darcy to be dead.

Darcy's laughter pulled Mera from her thoughts. Mera realized Darcy was reading them. "Very good, girl, very good.

Once I got inside her mind, I found the precious secret she was hiding. You." Darcy looked at Mera, her eyes full of affection. She smiled at Mera. And then they were back in the Astral Convergence again, Mera's stomach lurching.

"You were just like me, and I had to have you. But of course, by the time I discovered that truth, they had taken you. To her."

A bolt of lightning struck the ground between them. Mera flew backward as the grass caught fire. Darcy only laughed.

"I knew Ida would discover what you were. That she would destroy you as she had done to me. Don't you see, Mera?" Darcy cooed, renewed manic affection in her wide eyes. "I'm here to save you."

She moved closer, crossing the wall of fire on the ground in front of them. Mera crawled backward, struggling to get to her feet.

"I can show you what it means to be an Aether. Together, we will be the most powerful beings in the history of the world, any world. We could be a family, Mera. Your mother, too."

"If you want to be a family, why won't you just let my mother go?" Mera pressed, as she pushed herself up to stand again.

Darcy sighed. "Your mother doesn't understand my vision for you. But she will, in time. For now, I have to help her understand."

Something in Mera's brain clicked into place. "You needed her to get through the barrier around the village."

Darcy clapped her hands together. "My star pupil! It took me some time to build the power I needed to maintain constant control over Genevieve's mind, let alone the power required to take on Ida. But yes, my plan was to use your mother to help me gain entry into the village. But it wasn't until I sent her in that I realized the barrier was weak enough for me to go through myself," Darcy laughed, as if this was one big joke. "Who knew?"

"Okay, you got what you wanted. You can let my mother go now."

"Not yet, lovey. But I promise you I will soon."

Darcy took another step toward her, and Mera continued to move away. She was aware of how close to the cliff she was getting. In a few more steps, there would be nowhere to go but down.

"When?" Mera demanded, her anger flaring up inside of her.

"When Ida is dead."

"No!"

Another bolt of lightning struck behind Darcy, making Mera jump back.

"Ida will only stand in our way. They all will. They will take everything that you are away from you. They are cruel, small, and weak, and they can't be trusted with anything special. And we will end them—together."

"I won't help you." Mera reached the edge of the cliff—she was out of room and out of time.

"My dear, do you think you have a choice?"

Mera felt a cold pressure build on her skull.

It's easier this way, Mera. The pressure tightened, moving in through her nostrils. Her mind was going numb, succumbing to Darcy's power the way one dies of the cold—

shutting down little by little before everything goes dark.

Let me in, Darcy's will ripped at her mind.

Mera opened her mouth to scream, but nothing came out. She clenched her eyes shut. It was like when the Draugr was taking her over, only Darcy was so much stronger. It had been the sound of her mother's voice that had helped her throw off the Draugr. Her mother, who had always given her strength and protected her, even sacrificing herself to do so.

"*Mera*," a familiar voice whispered—the woman with the streak of white hair from her dream. The dream she woke from after being tossed off the cliff.

"*It's time to wake up now, dear.*"

It wasn't a dream, Mera realized. It was a message.

Mera knew what she had to do—something that, in reality, she would never come back from. But in this astral world, reality was what she made it.

Mera took a deep breath and stepped backward off the cliff.

"*Mera!*" Darcy's voice thundered as Mera fell away from her.

As she plummeted, Mera's energy bubbled into her head, like uncorked champagne. Light erupted in Mera's mind, blinding her, as the world shifted to her will.

Mera's eyes flew open. She was back in the Convergence in the real world. Darcy spun around, utterly bewildered.

Mera raised her hands and let out a wrathful wave of energy that crested and foamed as it left her. It collided with an unprepared Darcy, sending her flying backward.

Mera's attack reached Darcy before Ida's could. Vihaan reappeared and joined Patrick and Mrs. Hall in gaping at Mera.

Mera looked at her grandmother, and they started toward one another, but they had only gone a few steps before Darcy was on her feet. With a sweep of her hand, Darcy knocked Vihaan, Patrick, and Mrs. Hall to the ground. Vihaan's head bounced off a rock with a sickening thud.

"This is a family matter, wouldn't you say?" Darcy called out to them.

Ida squared to face Darcy while Mera kept moving toward Ida.

Darcy unleashed her energy at the same time as Ida. Both streams sliced through the air, then exploded upon impact. A thunderstorm erupted, and rain came down in buckets. The wind howled.

"You won't beat me again," Darcy called out over the noise of the storm.

Ida responded with a wave of her hand. The rain around Darcy sizzled, boiling. It struck Darcy's skin, and Darcy cried out. She froze the rain around Ida into bullet-sized hail. The pieces careened toward Ida, but she put up her shield, and they all bounced off.

Mera moved behind Ida, unseen by either of the sisters. Mrs. Hall tended to Vihaan while Patrick was sneaking closer to Genevieve.

"*Genevieve!*" Darcy's voice shrieked.

A switch flipped in Genevieve's mind. She snapped her head in Patrick's direction and sent a bolt of energy at him. He dodged, throwing himself to the ground. She advanced on him without hesitation.

"Mom, no!" Mera sprinted toward her mother. Genevieve raised her hand to strike at Patrick, but Mera sent out her own energy and wrapped it around her mother's wrist, preventing her from moving it.

Genevieve's head snapped toward her. She lifted her other hand and struck at Mera instead. Mera put up her shield, bracing herself against the impact. It almost knocked her over, but she dug her heels in, determined to stay upright.

When she looked up again, her mother was advancing on her.

"Mom, please, stop!" Mera tried putting her will into her voice, but the look in her mother's eyes made her heart plummet. It was as though she didn't even recognize Mera.

Genevieve stopped short. Patrick was on his feet again, his hands extended, neutralizing Genevieve with his powers. Genevieve balled her hands into fists and pulled her arms to her chest, then extended them, sending heat out all around her. It seared Mera's skin as it hit her, and Mera heard Patrick cry out before he hit the ground.

Genevieve turned to advance on Patrick. Mera sent out her energy around her ankles, tripping her. Genevieve fell to the ground, turning to look back at Mera, her eyes full of rage.

"Mom, it's me! It's Mera!" Mera willed her mother with all her strength. Darcy blocked her, her hold on her mother not lessened by her divided attention.

As Genevieve stood again, Patrick took hold of her with his neutralizing powers once more. His hands balled into fists as he tightened his grip. The pain on her mother's face stabbed at Mera's heart.

"Don't hurt her!" Mera screamed at Patrick.

"I won't," Patrick assured her, and she believed him. His expression darkened, and Mera followed his gaze.

Darcy was standing over Ida, her hands extended toward her sister, as she pulled shimmering ribbons of Ida's energy out of her and into her own body.

"*No!*"

Mera's energy surged out of her and flew at Darcy, hitting her like a tsunami. It sent her to the ground once again. Mera ran, feeling the wind itself accelerating her forward, getting her in between Ida and Darcy faster than she thought possible.

Darcy rose to her feet, muddy and infuriated.

"This is your choice then, Mera? You choose her over your own mother? Over yourself?" Darcy panted.

Darcy's skin glowed a neon blue. She was in a state of incredible strength. She had just fed, as Ida had described it, replenished her energy by stealing another's.

Mera let her own power build within her. That was Ida's energy Darcy had stolen. Darcy had no right to it.

The air froze. Mera's body breathed in the surrounding energy, pooling it in every cell of her being.

Darcy watched her with a hungry fascination. "So be it," she hissed.

Mera's body trembled. The air was so thin, she could barely draw breath.

As Darcy stepped forward, Mera let herself exhale, releasing every ion of energy she had within her just as Darcy did the same.

A gale of icy daggers formed in midair. They rushed toward Darcy, meeting her own blast in the middle. Ice erupted everywhere, billowing out and freezing the ground, which rumbled and cracked beneath them.

Mera held out her hands, keeping the iceberg of energy

from bouncing back at her. Mera's hands and arms froze, and her feet slipped on the frosted grass. Hail pelted Mera all over, and she had to shut her eyes to protect them from it.

Mera's teeth chattered as she clenched them together. She took in a breath, searching for more energy around her to take in, but found none. It rushed toward Darcy instead. Mera dug in her heels as hard as she could, using every bit of strength she had left, screaming with the effort.

Mera, give me your hand, Ida spoke into her mind.

Mera extended her hand back, and Ida took it. Ida's warmth flowed through her, boiling water in her frozen veins. Mera's eyes snapped open, and everything took on an ethereal blue glow, as though the world were underwater.

Mera unleashed pure lava from her steaming palm. The lava roared as it melted the impenetrable wall of frozen energy in front of her. Darcy shrieked as Mera's energy latched onto her, wrapping around her torso like a rope and forcing her hands to her sides.

Mera called to Ida's energy inside of Darcy's body. It answered—warm, strong, and constant—and seeped into the rope of energy. It moved into Mera's outstretched hand, flowed up her arm, through her chest, and down the other arm, before going back to its rightful home—Ida.

Reunited with her essence, Ida collapsed, breaking their connection and Mera's hold on Darcy.

"Ida!" Mera fell to Ida's side, but Ida was unconscious.

Darcy was on her knees, out of breath. Darcy glanced to her left then made a beeline for Mera's mother, who was still being held by Patrick.

"No!" Mera yelled, running after her.

Darcy flicked her hand toward an unprotected Patrick, throwing him backward. She took hold of Genevieve and vanished in a flash.

Mera ran through the air they had just been occupying, stunned.

The storm had ended. Darcy was gone. And so was her mother.

THIRTY

MERA STARED AT the spot where her mother disappeared. She turned to ask the others if they had seen the same thing, but their expressions made the words die in her throat.

Vihaan was sitting by Patrick's side, supported by Mrs. Hall. Mrs. Hall worked to heal Patrick, and his eyes fluttered open, back to consciousness.

"You're an Aether," Vihaan said, his voice cracking and weak.

"Yes," Mera replied, holding his gaze. She wasn't sure what she saw in it. Fear? Awe? Pity? She saw Ida was still lying on the ground. She rushed over to her and kneeled by her side.

They knew about her now. She didn't have room to worry about what was going to happen to her. She was too full of fear for her mother and Ida.

Mrs. Hall knelt on the other side of Ida. She put one hand on Ida's head and one on her chest and shut her eyes.

"There's something—off. Her energy. It's out of balance," Mrs. Hall said with her eyes still closed.

"Darcy tried to drain her. Well, she did. But I . . . got her energy back," Mera explained, stuttering.

At least, that's what she thought had happened. That's what it had felt like.

Mrs. Hall nodded, opening her eyes and looking at Mera. "You did a wonderful job. She needs to reconnect with her energy. If you hadn't gotten it back into her, she would have died."

"We need to get them out of here," Vihaan stated, struggling to stand.

"I can take them," Ani's voice called as she emerged from the woods and approached. Wyatt and Mr. Hall followed. Wyatt was staring at Mera, his expression full of concern.

"Ani," Vihaan reproached.

"Grandpa, I got this, okay?"

Ani put her hand on Ida's shoulder. She reached up to Mera, and Mera saw her eyes were full of tears. Mera took her friend's hand, and the three of them swirled away.

***

It took three days for Ida to wake up, and they were the longest of Mera's life. Mrs. Hall stayed in the guest bedroom next to Ida's, tending to her as she slept. Mera perched in the reading chair next to Ida's bed, allowed to stay home from school as her grandmother recovered. Mera spent the time tracking the sun's journey across the bedroom through the windows, lost in thought about Ida and her mother.

Her only moments of solace were the brief daily visits with Ani and Wyatt, who came by with Vihaan and Mr. Hall to check in on Ida and bring food. The three of them sat together on the downstairs couch, Ani and Wyatt bringing her schoolwork and updates from town.

Since their energies connected on the beach, being near them encased Mera in warmth. She leaned backward into the soft couch and the comfort of their bond as Ani and Wyatt argued about which of their Elements had been more effective at defeating the rogue Terras. When they left each day, Mera returned to Ida's bedside.

Mera had been staring at Ida's face, thinking it seemed more flushed than it had in recent days, when her eyes fluttered open. Mera let out an involuntary shriek of surprise. Ida winced and then cast a slow, purposeful look of judgment upon her granddaughter.

"Ah," she rasped, "what a soothing reception."

"You scared me!" Mera cried.

"When you've pulled it together, some water would be lovely," Ida said, her voice cracking.

Though she was her grandmother, Ida had never registered as old to Mera before, but in the soft afternoon light, her wrinkles seemed etched in the shadows on her pearlescent skin, the bags under her eyes darker and heavier.

It took several days for Ida to be strong enough to stand. Bundling themselves against the whipping ocean wind, Mera took her on slow walks around the yard. Being outside had a marked improvement on Ida. The color in her cheeks returned as she breathed in the salty sea air.

One morning, they both woke before dawn and ventured out to the bench between the willow trees and took a seat. Ida closed her eyes, and they sat in silence for a long time, until Ida broke it.

"Tell me. I'm ready."

Mera told Ida everything—how Darcy had stolen Ida's

energy and Mera had taken it back. How Darcy had somehow vanished, Genevieve in tow.

Ida closed her eyes but nodded.

"We will get her back, Mera. Genevieve is strong. We will fight for her, as she will fight for us. That is our bond."

Mera knew the words were true as Ida spoke them. Darcy would return to Convergence, which meant her mother would, as well. Mera promised herself she'd free her mother from Darcy's mental grip. She just had to be ready when the time came, but she wouldn't be able to do it alone.

Mera looked up at Ida again. Ida took her hand.

"They caught Rochester," Mera said, wanting to give her grandmother good news. "Pretty quickly, actually. They found him trying to hole up in a cave below the Convergence. Got flushed out by the high tide."

Ida let out a small cackle that turned into a cough.

"He's being held in town somewhere. His location is a secret, just in case he still has any followers out there."

"I only wish I was the one who found him," Ida said, a steeliness back in her voice.

Another moment of silence followed.

"They know I'm an Aether," Mera said, her stomach in knots.

"Who does?" Ida's head snapped toward her.

"The Halls. Vihaan. Patrick. Vihaan said they would keep it a secret. For now, at least."

Ida sighed. "They will."

"It can't stay a secret forever. Everyone knows Darcy is back. Ani and Wyatt say the town is freaking out. It's all Vihaan can do to keep the peace." The words fell out of her in a panic. And then came the question she had been too afraid to think about since it had all happened. "What will they do when they find out about me?"

"I will never let anything happen to you, Mera," Ida squeezed her hand.

"But they're afraid, you said so yourself. What happened with Darcy—"

"Whatever their fears," Ida interjected, "you are the only person strong enough to protect us from her now."

"But that's not true. It was our connection that gave me the strength to fight her."

"Yes, but that connection lives in you, Mera," Ida reminded her. "Or have you not been listening to anything I've taught you?"

Mera rolled her eyes but smiled. "So, what's going to happen now?"

"That I don't know. But whatever happens, we'll face it together."

Ida rose and squeezed Mera's hand before pulling her up with her.

"Let's go inside." Ida put her arm, sturdy again, around Mera's shoulder.

As the sun cracked open the sky and rose in full, the first beams of the day's light fell on the house, cascading over the windows and illuminating them in a shimmering glow. The weathervane shifted with the changing wind as the morning rays highlighted the faded brushstrokes of paint on the house's facade.

Mera leaned into Ida, strong enough to lead the way again, as they walked the path carved by the generations before them. Mera followed her grandmother up the front steps and through the door, finally home.

EPILOGUE

IT WAS MORE than she ever hoped. She played what she had seen over in her mind as she crept away from the tree line and back to her car.

She knew the girl was powerful—she experienced her power up close. But she never dreamed the girl was . . .

She parked her car and sat inside it for a long time, lost in the possibilities unfolding in front of her. She was light-headed from the excitement of it all, and now, having the honor to bring what she saw back to the others.

After years of being spurned, rejected, outcast, they would welcome her back with open arms. No—they would celebrate her.

For she had seen not only the return of The Exalted One. But discovered a second Exalted One had been delivered to them.

She saw it again—Darcy and Mera facing off against one another, power unleashed in all its glory. The charged chill emanating from them spread all the way to the trees she had hidden behind. The memory of it brought tears to her eyes.

"A blessed day," she whispered to herself as she

undid her seatbelt and climbed out of her car.

As she made her way up the sidewalk toward the house, she shivered. Mera's return to Convergence was a sign of the glory to come—it was a miracle.

She reached out and knocked on the door, gathering herself.

The door opened, and a figure peered out at her.

"The time has come," Ms. Hughes said, a smile creeping onto her lips. "The Exaltation has begun."

About the Authors

 Rebecca and Katherine Lewis are sisters who were born in a small town on the Connecticut coast.

 Rebecca attended Emerson College, where she studied Creative Writing and English. Working in education, she has taught and built curriculum for children from the Mississippi Delta to Massachusetts to Texas. She is currently studying Educational Leadership, Organizations, and Entrepreneurship at Harvard University.

 Katherine has a BFA in Film & Television Production from NYU's Tisch School of the Arts and an MFA in Writing for Screen & Television from USC's School of Cinematic Arts. Living in Los Angeles, CA, she works in production management on children's content and has writing credits on kid's shows for PBS and Netflix.

Made in the USA
Middletown, DE
29 August 2021